The Legend of Evelyn
Tessa Marie

Lilac Ivy Books

Library of Congress Control Number: 2024921534

ISBNs
979-8-9916626-0-4 (paperback)
979-8-9916626-1-1 (hardcover)

First edition 2025

For my little brother. May you always find the adventure in life.

1

Sunday, September 1

Clarissa was a jack of all trades and a master of one. Some called it social manipulation; she preferred the terms insight and persuasion. She specialized in getting exactly what she wanted. Her friends, although jealous of her skills, appreciated her ability to talk them out of sticky situations. She was about to have to do it again.

Derek swung his fist at the stranger in front of him. He chose violence as a response to insults, as always. The bartender looked at Derek, then at Clarissa, desperately hoping she would control her drunk friend. The stranger punched back, hitting Derek in the face again, and again, and again. Derek didn't stand a chance. Clarissa shoved her way between the two, looking up at both of them, then speaking to the stranger. "Now listen, as we both know, my friend here is an idiot. I'm sorry you had to put up with him; trust me, I've been putting up with him for a while, and I know how difficult it can be. How about he buys you a drink, we leave peacefully, and you can go back to enjoying your evening?" Clarissa tossed the bartender a gold coin and left, dragging Derek behind her.

The pair headed towards a large oak tree on the outskirts of town, the designated meeting spot where they could hopefully find the rest of their friends. They were the first to make it to the tree; the others probably didn't have their escapades interrupted by drunken fistfights. Jemma came next, and it didn't take a dice roll to notice the mischievous grin on the teenage girl's face. She held in her hands a small golden ruby ring.

"Please tell me you didn't steal that from the shop we visited earlier," Clarissa begged.

Jemma shrugged. "I could tell you I didn't steal it, or I could tell you the truth. Your choice."

Clarissa sighed. Jemma seemed to cause trouble in every town they visited, but her skills were useful, and the group desperately needed her, so they couldn't simply ditch her like Clarissa wanted.

After an hour of silently watching the stars, Clarissa heard footsteps approaching. She sat up quickly to see Jareth and Elijah. "You made it back! Did you get it? Did they see you? Are you hurt?"

"Calm down, princess," Eli said with an eye roll, walking past her to check on Derek, who was asleep under the tree.

Jareth smiled at Clarissa. "Yes, we got the scrolls. And we're unharmed. No one even noticed us." He sat beside her and handed her a small box. "How was your evening?"

"Well, I kept Derek alive, but I couldn't keep Jemma's sticky fingers away from that jewelry shop." She ran her fingers over the carved details of the box in her hands. Obtaining it was the whole reason they had come to this small town in the first place. The goal had been accomplished, yet she still felt like a failure.

"Everyone is alive and healthy. I'd consider that a success." Jareth put a comforting hand on her shoulder, then walked away.

"You set up camp and rest for the night. And we'll end the game there for tonight," David said.

Evelyn laughed. "You try to start a fight every single session!" she yelled at Aaron.

Aaron simply shrugged. "What's the point of this game if I don't get to start fake fights?"

"What about making friends, fighting monsters, uncovering mysteries, saving the world..."

"I still prefer fist fights." Aaron grinned, which made Evelyn laugh. He had always enjoyed the combat part of the game, rolling the dice and desperately hoping for high enough numbers to win the fight. Evelyn, on the other hand, enjoyed the story. Clarissa was a character that she got to play in a fantasy world that David created. Likewise, her friends created their own characters, and together, they wove a narrative full of depth and meaning and chaos.

Aaron dumped all his dice into a plastic bag and tossed it into his backpack, in strong contrast to Oliver next to him, who meticulously placed every dice in its slot in his case. Evelyn cleaned up her own dice and books, then, with Liam's help, cleared the empty pizza boxes and paper plates off the table.

"You should go home soon. You have a PDEs test in the morning, right?" Liam said.

"Yeah, unfortunately."

"I'm sure you'll ace it."

"It's partial differential equations. No one aces it."

Liam smiled and handed her her backpack. "You always say that, and you always still manage to get an A. I'm sure you'll do great."

She put on her boots and walked to the door. She didn't want to leave so soon, but Liam was right. Her test in the morning called for a lot of studying and a bit of sleep. "Bye, guys! I'll see you next week!" she shouted.

"Goodbye, princess," Oliver yelled from the other room.

She rolled her eyes with a grin on her face and walked out of the house.

As Evelyn entered her small campus apartment, she was overwhelmed by the mess. Dirty bowls and pans were scattered around the kitchen from her cupcake attempts for Aaron's birthday. The whiteboards on the wall were filled with math problems with more wrong solutions than right. Textbooks and notes were scattered around the room in disarray. She desperately needed to clean, but more desperately, she needed to study. She closed the door to the kitchen, shoved everything in her closet, and once the mess was successfully out of her sight, she went to work.

Math was a hard subject to study. It took the right mixture of memorization, practice, and endurance. In high school, every problem had one right answer, one simple and consistent process taught by the teacher and practiced with plenty of homework problems. In college, the solutions to math questions were more like one-page essays, solving the heat equation or proving that the square root of two is irrational, and rarely did students solve the question correctly on the first attempt. It was no surprise that Calculus 1 was one of the classes that freshmen commonly failed.

Evelyn, however, was no freshman. She was a senior, and she wasn't ready to let partial differential equations ruin her 4.0 GPA.

She set up her laptop with the professor's slides, pulled out her carefully designed notecards of formulas and theorems, and opened her textbook to Chapter 1. Then she grabbed a dry-erase marker and began to work.

Monday, September 2

The golden sunlight shone through the dreamy white clouds and cascaded over the exhausted girl walking through campus in sweatpants and pushing her tangled mess of hair away from her tired eyes. Her test had gone seemingly well, although success had cost her a good night of sleep and ten dollars for two cups of coffee. At least the next hour of her schedule—book club—was relatively easy.

During her first year of college, her freshman seminar professor forced everyone to join two campus organizations: one academic and one extracurricular. She quit competition math after a semester, but she stayed in the book club. It was nice to read something other than a textbook. They picked a new book every month, the genres varying widely, from young adult fantasy to historical memoirs.

"Evelyn! Hi!" Erica spotted her from across the building and ran to catch up. "Are you excited for book club today? I finished the poetry book last night. The last poem was so amazing, about how all good things must come to an end, alluding to the ending of the book. I'm sure Beckett loved it; he's always had an obsession with poetry. Honestly, he'll probably talk the whole meeting and none of us will even get to say a... Evelyn?"

"What?" She forced her eyes back open. "...sorry, I zoned out. Just a little tired."

"You look like a zombie."

"I need a cup of coffee."

"You need a nap."

"I have book club, two classes, dinner with Caroline, and then two long math assignments. Coffee will have to suffice," Evelyn said as they entered the classroom together.

Book club had already begun. There were discussion prompts on the whiteboards and ballots on the table to vote for the best poem. Students had formed circles of chairs for conversation. Beckett gestured towards two empty chairs in his group, and Evelyn and Erica joined him.

"—and the last poem was sort of an allegory written to you as the reader right before you finish the book, reminding you that once you close the final page, you'll never get the joy of reading the book for the first time again," Beckett said. "It was really sad."

"But there will always be more books to read 'for the first time'," Melanie said.

"That's true, but will any ever be as good as this book? What if every book we read is just worse than the last?"

"But there are infinitely many books. There's guaranteed to be a book better than this one."

"That's not exactly how infinity works," Evelyn chimed in.

"Okay, math major," Melanie responded. Evelyn wasn't sure if the comment was meant to be a joke or an insult, but she stayed silent for the rest of the hour.

At the end of the meeting, they voted on the next book to read, and after a long debate full of constant objections, they finally settled on a newly released fantasy novel. Then Melanie handed out manuscript copies of her new book. Every week, at least one student had a new manuscript ready for editing, like writing a novel was the unofficial capstone for the English majors that composed the majority of the club.

"Do you want a copy? I'd appreciate your feedback." Melanie held out a stack of papers towards Evelyn.

"Sure, I'll read it for you." Evelyn took the manuscript.

"Great, thank you so much!" Melanie wandered off to find her next editor.

Evelyn glanced through the papers. She wasn't sure how much help she could offer. The novel was probably perfect, just like everything else in Melanie's life. Her perfectly curled hair, perfectly curated outfits, and perfectly designed social media profiles irked Evelyn for a reason she couldn't quite pinpoint.

"Maybe I could write a book too," Erica said. "It sounds like fun."

"I'll edit it for you if you do, but don't overwork yourself. It's your first semester of college. You haven't even learned to drive yet; there's no rush to become a published author," Evelyn said. Erica was a prodigy child, graduating high school a month before her 17th birthday. If she could get into med school, she could start her residency at just 24 years old, and with her intelligence, she could probably attend any school she wanted. She knew everything there was to know about biology and chemistry, but her academic skills far outshone her practical skills. Evelyn still had to teach her how to cook a grilled cheese and run the clothes washer in the dorm room.

"Maybe I'll work on it over Christmas break," Erica said. "How was game night last night?"

"Well, no one died, so that's good."

"In the game or in real life?"

"Both."

"I'm glad." Erica laughed. "Your friends are chaotic."

"You know you're one of my friends, right?"

"Oh, I know." Erica smiled. "I'm going to miss you when you graduate. You'll probably go off to some Ivy League law school and ditch me."

"I haven't even started my applications yet. Besides, we'll keep in touch. You can always call me when you forget how to preheat the oven." She glanced at her phone. "You know your chem class starts in 3 minutes, right? Isn't that the one with the rude professor?"

Erica glanced at her watch. "Oh no... okay, I'll see you later!" She sprinted off to avoid the wrath of her chemistry professor.

Evelyn sat down at a table in the library and opened her topology textbook. If she could push through a couple hours of studying, then two more classes, she could finally rest and get dinner with Caroline.

It was going to be a long day.

As the sun set, Evelyn walked across campus to meet up with Caroline. Caroline had graduated a few years ago, but her favorite restaurant was still the burger place on the corner of campus. Evelyn arrived first and ordered burgers for both of them: two double bacon burgers and two servings of sweet potato fries. Evelyn had been copying Caroline's order since the day they started meeting there.

She sat down at a small table in the corner and started scrolling on her phone while she waited. She scrolled through family photos and "life hacks" and funny videos—

"What are you looking at?"

She almost jumped out of her seat when she heard Caroline behind her, spying on her phone screen over her shoulder. Somehow, Caroline had walked through the front door without Evelyn noticing.

Caroline laughed at the scene. "Get off your phone. Your order's ready; they called your name a minute ago."

Evelyn grabbed their food from the counter and sat back down. "You know, most people would just walk in and say hi, not try to sneak up and scare me."

"Most people are boring." Caroline took a bite of her burger. "I missed this place. We haven't been here in a while. I haven't seen you much outside of game nights."

"Life has been busy. I spent all summer working at my internship and studying for the LSAT. Now I just need to wait for my score and keep my grades up."

"You'll do great. Don't stress."

"That's easy for you to say. You've already graduated and gotten a job."

"That won't fix all your problems, kiddo. Eat some more sweet potato fries. They'll make you feel better."

"They make everything better," Evelyn said as she grabbed a handful of them. She had missed her conversations with Caroline and their discussions about gaming and boys and life. They lost track of time and talked until nightfall, when Evelyn headed off to finish the two assignments that had been invading her thoughts all day, like parasites that wouldn't leave until she hit the online "Submit" button.

The honors lounge was the intersection of pure genius and absolute stupidity. The whiteboards were filled with a mixture of complicated chemistry problems and borderline-offensive jokes. The room was scattered with textbooks, laptops, fidget toys, and rubber ducks. A girl in the corner played ukulele, while some students at a table worked on a group project, and others gathered around a computer to watch a short film they made. Nonetheless, the honors lounge was Evelyn's favorite study spot. The mayhem simply added to its charm.

She cleared off a table and set up her laptop, putting on headphones to block out the noise. She opened her first assignment and started on question one of five.

By the end of the first hour, she had moved on to question two.

There was no way to finish these assignments at a reasonable hour, and the coffee from earlier had already worn off. Maybe she could finish just one more question. She scribbled equations, paused, scratched out the work, and tried again. The page filled with attempt after attempt.

By the end of the third hour, she still hadn't finished question two.

Evelyn hated giving up. She liked to finish assignments; she found satisfaction in completion and contentment in marking tasks off of her to-do list, but with no possibility of finishing, she walked home at one in the morning, the parasites still invading her thoughts.

Thursday, September 5

The fire alarm was not a pleasant sound. The time of day—3 a.m.—made it even less pleasant.

Evelyn trudged into her living room with a blanket wrapped around her. Her roommate Bethany looked at the living room smoke detector with pure hatred. "I have the umbrella. Do you have your car keys?"

Evelyn nodded. She was prepared; this was not her first middle-of-the-night fire alarm, and unfortunately, it probably wasn't her last.

The girls walked outside, making their way through the flood of exiting students and into the pouring rain. They ran across the parking lot, but even their nice umbrella couldn't keep them from getting soaked.

Evelyn sat in the driver's seat. "It'll take about 15 minutes for the fire truck to get here, and then 30 minutes for them to inspect the dorm and shut the alarm off. What do we want to do in the meantime?"

"I'm a little hungry, but there's probably nothing open this time of night."

"You have so much to learn, young one." Evelyn handed the freshman her phone with a list of 24/7 restaurants she had compiled over the past few years. "Take your pick."

They settled on a taco restaurant with a drive-through and headed across town. Evelyn let Bethany choose the music and ended up listening to an eclectic mix of acoustic songs and video game soundtracks.

"Aren't you going to miss 3 a.m. taco runs when you graduate?" Bethany asked.

"Maybe. But I won't miss the 3 a.m. fire alarms."

"At least I don't have early morning classes today. Do you?"

"Not classes, just assignments to work on."

They ordered their tacos, and a half-asleep employee handed them a bag. "These are absolutely delicious," Bethany said with her mouth full of food. "You're a genius."

"I'm just experienced," Evelyn replied. "Only the best restaurants make it on my list."

"It seems like you have everything in life figured out. I don't know what I'll do without you next year. I'll have some random boring roommate who doesn't appreciate midnight tacos."

"I'll miss you too." Evelyn sighed, but her sadness didn't stem from missing Bethany, although she would. Bethany truly believed Evelyn had solved every mystery life presented. Evelyn felt the exact opposite. She didn't have a law school lined up yet, so she didn't even know what city she would move to after graduation. She wasn't sure how to afford tuition and housing. On top of that, this entire plan relied on her LSAT score, which was yet to be released, and even if her LSAT score was nearly perfect, she still had a lot to figure out. She didn't know how to make a budget, much less open a 401k. She wasn't even sure she understood what a 401k was. Her social life was even more stressful than her financial life. She hated making new friends; it drained her social battery constantly. Maybe that's why she hadn't been on a date in over 3 years...

Her spiral of thoughts was interrupted by the vibrating of her phone. The building group chat announced that the fire alarm had been shut off.

"Guess it's time to head back," Bethany said. "We'll have to investigate in the morning to find who set off the fire alarm. It was probably Jerry again. Someone needs to tell him to stop burning pizzas in the middle of the night."

The girls drove back home, their stomachs filled with tacos, ears filled with music, and voices filled with laughter.

Friday, September 6

For Evelyn, Fridays were a day of peaceful productivity. Her schedule was void of classes and responsibilities, which meant she had plenty of time to cross objectives off of her growing to-do list. The best way to accomplish that, Evelyn had discovered, was with boba tea.

She walked into the small tea shop with her laptop bag in hand and waved at the barista. "Hey, Piper!"

"Good morning! Strawberry green tea with crystal boba?" Piper asked, reciting Evelyn's typical order from memory.

"Of course." Evelyn swiped her card to pay for the drink. "How's life? How's the new puppy?"

"Absolutely adorable! Here, I'll show you a picture." She pulled out her phone, and the girls picked up the conversation where they had left it last Friday. Piper had worked every Friday at the boba shop for the last two years, and catching up with her had become a regular part of Evelyn's routine.

The girls scrolled through pictures of the puppy until another customer walked in, and Piper went back to work. Evelyn took her drink and found an empty table, a relatively easy task in the quiet little shop. She set up her laptop, opened up her organized to-do list, and took a deep breath.

Email her professor with a question about the homework. Check.

Fix the formatting (and spelling) (and grammar) on the slides for the dreaded group project. Check.

Fill out the membership forms for the book club. Check.

Take the partial differential equations concepts quiz.

She sighed. The other tasks had been quick, easy, and painless. This one was going to take a while.

Every week, in addition to their normal homework, tests, and pop quizzes, her PDEs professor made students take an online multiple-choice quiz covering concepts learned that week. The "multiple-choice" aspect was the only redeeming quality. The questions had up to ten answer choices, and students had to pick all the answers that were correct. Every elementary test strategy, like the process of elimination, was completely inapplicable.

The intimidating "Begin" button at the bottom of the quiz instructions stared her down until she finally built up the courage to press it.

The first question popped up, and right on cue, her phone rang.

She dug through her backpack to shut off the loud ringing interrupting the quietness of the tea shop. After a painful few seconds, she finally managed to turn off her phone, and she tried her best to refocus her attention on the quiz.

She hit "Submit" with only seconds left on the clock. Her grade was still unknown, but she was grateful to be finished. She could wait until next week to worry about the next one.

She pulled out her phone to see a missed call from Liam and a text.

Liam:

> hey evelyn! did you know it's oliver's birthday tomorrow? we're celebrating on sunday. can you bake a cake?

Evelyn had forgotten about Oliver's birthday, but it was no surprise Liam remembered; he loved birthdays more than anyone she had ever met. He threw surprise parties for every birthday in their friend group, although the consistency meant it wasn't much of a surprise anymore. Liam loved cake and candles and celebrations, and he always knew exactly what present each person would want. Evelyn, on the other hand, never understood birthdays. Turning a year older just seemed like a natural part of life, not a special occasion to be celebrated. Nonetheless, Liam's pure-hearted enthusiasm made her smile. She added "Bake a birthday cake for Oliver" to her to-do list. Then she took another sip of her strawberry tea and continued her work.

Saturday, September 7

Evelyn woke up to her alarm at 7 a.m.

It was the same as every other day. She begrudgingly pushed aside her soft gray blanket and climbed out of her lofted college dorm bed. With black pants, a white shirt, and a green blazer in hand, she walked to her bathroom to get ready for another day.

She braided her long blonde hair into the same style as always, two braids on each side of her head that merged into one. She put in her contacts to fix her minor nearsightedness, brushed her teeth, and got dressed for another day at her part-time job as a receptionist at a local law firm. Her work consisted mostly of answering phone calls with repetitive responses like "I'm sorry, he's not here today. He'll be back on Monday." or "Yes, I can pass on a message for you." or "No, this isn't the pizza shop. Their phone number ends in a four, not a five."

The day was just like the Saturday before it and the Saturday that would come after. She had survived yet another week, just like she would next week, and the next, until after 16 weeks, the semester ended. Then a new semester would begin, and her routine would be reset yet still the same, day after day, week after week, semester after semester, until one day, hopefully, by grace alone, she would graduate law school.

It was in the breaks that she found happiness and rest. The break between semesters, whether summer vacation or Christmas with her family, was always a nice, clear interruption to her schedule. Although less noticeable, the breaks between days and weeks were peaceful as well. The few minutes scrolling social media in bed every night made her feel like, for a moment, time wasn't real. Due dates faded from existence, and midterms were just hypothetical. It allowed her thoughts to ponder something other than the never-ending to-do list that dictated each day and each hour of her life. Every night, she had a few minutes to scroll on her phone and forget about the world, and every week, she had a few hours at game night to do the same, to immerse herself in a fictional fantasy that was much more interesting than her mundane routine. Evelyn was a normal student at a normal college living a normal life, but Clarissa was the heroine every young girl strived to be. She was strong, brave, intelligent, and a good friend, loved and adored by anyone and everyone who met her. Her life was always an adventure; there was no schedule, no routine, no required jobs other than the responsibility she placed upon herself to save the world. Clarissa was the protagonist of her own story, and every week, before returning to her daily routine like a broken record, Evelyn got to play a game to write the next chapter of that story.

THE PARTY

Elijah Praetor (Oliver's Character) - *a fighter who believes anything is possible*
    Strengths: intimidation, stubbornness
    Weaknesses: intimidation, stubbornness
    Skills: strength, sword fighting

Jareth Amans (Liam's Character) - *a wizard who underestimates his own power*
    Strengths: intelligence, honesty
    Weaknesses: hesitancy, anxiety
    Skills: magic, disguises

Clarissa Amica (Evelyn's Character) - *a kind companion who prefers words to weapons*
    Strengths: affableness, insight
    Weaknesses: clumsiness, fragility
    Skills: wisdom, persuasion

Derek Comicus (Aaron's Character) - *a medic who makes everyone smile*
    Strengths: steadfastness, reliability
    Weaknesses: rashness, ignorance
    Skills: hunting, survival

Jemma Proditor (Caroline's Character) - *a "former" thief who dearly loves her friends*
    Strengths: cheerfulness, nonchalance
    Weaknesses: duplicity, recklessness
    Skills: stealth, lock picking

2

Sunday, September 8

The party traveled together down the long dirt road to Caridelle, the famed capital of Arydia. They had each ended up on this journey through their own individual stories, but those were of less importance. They were now a team with one vital task at hand: return the box of scrolls to Kinsley Lister.

According to the mage that gave Jemma this quest, Kinsley was the daughter of one of the most prominent and wealthy families in Caridelle. Her parents were collectors of exquisite magical items from across the globe, and Kinsley had followed suit in building a collection of her own. However, her naivety led her to neglect proper security measures, allowing the box of scrolls to be stolen from her home. Supposedly, Kinsley would pay a small fortune for the return of these scrolls.

Since they had already acquired the box (which Elijah insisted on carrying himself), the remaining steps seemed simple. Eli was convinced that the rest would be easy, but Clarissa wasn't so certain. They still had to travel for another day to reach the city, then try to gain an audience with Kinsley, and assuming the mage was telling the truth—

Her thoughts were interrupted by Derek grabbing her shoulder and pointing to the bushes in front of them. She heard a rustling noise and took a step back. Elijah pushed past her with his sword unsheathed, and Derek drew his bow.

Suddenly, the wolves attacked. She was expecting two or three animals, maybe four, but in an instant, there were too many to count, coming from different bushes in different directions. Elijah swung his sword at one, and Derek shot arrows at another. Jemma threw a bomb that caught the nearest bush on fire. Clarissa fumbled with a spell, trying her best to remember Jareth's teaching as a wolf ran at her. Just in time, she hit it in the face with a bright burst of energy. It collapsed to the ground, but her relief was short-lived. She felt a bite in the back of her calf as another wolf attacked from behind, dragging her back and knocking her off her feet. She tried another spell, but it failed. In her panicked state, she couldn't perfect the words and gestures, so she switched strategies. She pulled out a dagger from her belt and sliced at the animal's face as it dragged her back by the leg. The first cut missed, and the next barely drew blood. She threw the dagger, and it landed in the grass out of reach, not remotely close to hitting its target. She dug her fingers into the dirt for traction and jerked her captive leg away. The wolf's teeth ripped through the skin on her calf, shooting pain up her leg. She pulled free for only a moment until the wolf bit her other leg and continued dragging her. She grabbed another dagger from her belt and tried to slice at the wolf again, when suddenly, it froze. The wolf stared at her, its jaws still locked on her calf, but its eyes were full of terror. "Derek, I need your help here!" Jareth shouted, focusing on the wolf and the spell keeping it in place. Suddenly an arrow flew past him and hit the wolf in the side. It slumped to the ground, releasing its grip on Clarissa.

Jareth knelt beside her. "Hey, look at me. It's okay. Deep breaths. Breathe in"—he demonstrated for her—"and breathe out. Again." He took another deep breath, and Clarissa matched his rhythm, trying her best to push the pain out of her mind. "You'll be okay, Clarissa, I promise. It's just a few small cuts," Jareth said, looking at the contradicting trail of blood in the dirt in front of him.

"Hey, princess. Are you alright?" Elijah approached them. "Let's get you up, and Derek can take a look at the injuries. Jemma, can you put out the fire?"

"Don't move her; I don't want you getting dirt in the wounds," Derek yelled from across the road that had been transformed into a war zone, with blood, dead wolves, and weapons scattered on the ground.

Clarissa laid her head on her arms. "I'm so tired."

"Just rest. It's okay." Jareth placed a hand on her shoulder, and she closed her eyes.

It was impossible to sleep while her painful wounds were being wrapped in bandages. She tried her best to focus on the simple task of breathing, but the mental image of the fight replayed in her head. If only she could have performed the spells correctly, she might not have gotten so injured.

Derek bandaged her wounds, Elijah cleaned off the weapons, and Jemma extinguished the bush fire before it started another. Jareth gathered Clarissa's daggers while still keeping his eyes trained on her. The party tried their best to recuperate and relax before they inevitably started traveling again.

"And we'll take a break there for dinner!" David announced.

Liam leaned over to Evelyn, whispering. "You brought the cake, right? Is it in the fridge?" She nodded. "Wait here everyone, I have a surprise!" Liam ran off, and the group looked around in pretend confusion.

Liam came back with the cake a minute later, candles burning bright. He walked carefully, trying his best not to drop it and burn the house down. Oliver's eyes lit up. Evelyn wasn't sure if he genuinely thought the friend group would forget his birthday, or if he was just feigning amazement. The group sang "Happy Birthday" to Oliver before he blew out the candles.

"Okay, dinner time. There's pizza in the kitchen!" Liam announced.

"Meat lovers with thin crust?" Oliver asked.

"Did you really think I would forget your favorite?"

The group filled their plates with pizza and cake. There were balloons and presents, smiles and laughter. Evelyn took her unofficially assigned seat between Liam and Caroline at the table. They had been friends for only a couple of years, yet they had already formed habits and traditions and plenty of inside jokes. Evelyn and Aaron were the youngest—the only two still in college. They had met in their freshman seminar class and bonded over their mutual despise for their professor who took freshman seminar way too seriously. Then Aaron introduced Evelyn to Liam, a junior and Aaron's math tutor at the time. Liam introduced them to Oliver, his best friend since childhood, and David, his former college roommate. The five of them spent a lot of time together in those first few months, trying every board game they could find and watching every cringe-worthy movie released. Evelyn didn't mind being the only girl, but she was grateful for Caroline to join when she and David began dating. After the first date, Evelyn, Aaron, Liam, and Oliver fulfilled their self-appointed responsibility to interrogate her. Fortunately, Caroline passed their test, and she and Evelyn quickly became friends.

It was Caroline who introduced the group to tabletop role-playing games. She was their first game master, creating an intricate fantasy world for them to set their characters inside. After a few months, David took over the role so that Caroline could play. They built new characters, each distinct in personality and chaotic in unique ways. That was when Evelyn created Clarissa, the empathetic young girl who made friends with anyone she met. She was extraordinarily brave, immensely kind, and determined to save everyone at all times. She was everything Evelyn wished she could be.

Clarissa leaned on Elijah for support as she limped down the road. Her legs were badly injured, but Derek assured her the wounds would heal with time.

"Just another hour or so until we reach Caridelle," Eli promised.

As the sun began to set over the horizon, the walls of the city began to rise. "Name and business," a guard demanded as they reached the gate.

"Elijah Praetor. These are my friends Clarissa, Derek, Jareth, and Jemma. My friend here"—he gestured to Clarissa—"was badly injured by some wolves this morning, and we're just looking for a safe place to rest for the night."

"Just staying for one night?" the guard asked.

"Yes, sir. One night and we'll be on our way."

"Alright. Don't cause any trouble." The guard opened the gate and let them in.

The party entered the city in awe. They had been told many stories about the magnificent Caridelle, but words could not properly describe their surroundings.

The massive architecture seemed to violate the laws of physics. The crowded streets were packed with locals and adventurers, families with children running amok, and salesmen trying to hand them a newspaper or a snack. They passed taverns, potion shops, blacksmiths, and bakeries. Caridelle offered any flavor of consumerism one could wish for.

They found a small inn near the entrance of town with open rooms where they could rest for the night. Elijah helped Clarissa up the stairs, and she sat on the bed in her room while Derek replaced the bandages on her legs.

"The cuts look a lot better," Derek promised her. "You should be able to walk fairly well on your own tomorrow."

"Don't push yourself too hard, though. You can stay here and rest if you need," Jareth said.

Clarissa smiled at him. "Thank you, Jareth. But I think I'll be okay. It should be an easy day tomorrow."

"Get some rest. Elijah and I are going to scope out the city tonight. Derek and Jemma... where's Jemma?"

Clarissa sighed. They'd only been in Caridelle an hour and, of course, they'd already lost her. "I'll find her." She started to stand, but Derek stopped her.

"I'm not done with the bandages. Don't move yet."

"I'll go find her," Jareth said.

"Can't you just send her a message spell?" Derek asked.

"She never responds to those anyways," Jareth yelled over his shoulder as he left the room.

31

Derek finished with the bandages after a few minutes, then left Clarissa alone to rest, giving her plenty of time to sit in silence and worry. She had no clue where Jareth or Jemma was; she could only hope Jareth wasn't injured and Jemma wasn't in jail.

Eventually there was a knock at the door, and a small teenage girl entered slowly with a tiny vial in her hands. "I brought you some pain medicine," Jemma said.

"You stole it, didn't you?"

"Only to make you feel better." Jemma handed the vial to Clarissa then climbed into the other bed and hid under the blankets.

Clarissa sighed and cast a message spell to Jareth. 'She's back at the inn now, safe and sound.'

'Thanks, Claire. I'll see you for breakfast in the morning. Goodnight.'

She drank the medicine and laid down to rest, grateful that everyone was safe and hopeful that tomorrow would be a better day.

"Are we really going to end there? We don't get to meet Kinsley yet?" Caroline complained to David.

David shrugged. "You'll have to wait for next week."

Caroline rolled her eyes, pretending to be upset at her boyfriend, but she couldn't suppress the grin on her face.

"Can I keep the leftover cake?" Oliver asked.

"I'm pretty sure Aaron ate the last slice," Evelyn said.

Aaron entered the room with a mouth full of icing. "Are you talking about me?"

"I'll just have to wait for your birthday to get more cake then," Oliver said to Evelyn. "Isn't it coming up soon?"

"In four weeks," Liam interrupted, smiling at Evelyn. "How'd your PDEs test go?"

She shrugged. "It's finished, at least."

"That's a good thing. Do you have any more tests this week?"

Evelyn shook her head. "Just five classes, four homeworks, a quiz, and a project."

"Sometimes I miss college, and then I talk to you, Evelyn." He moved to the kitchen to throw away pizza boxes and cake plates.

Evelyn followed with more trash. "It must be nice to leave the office at five o'clock every day without homework to worry about."

"You'll get there one day. And then instead of homework, you'll have bills to pay and meals to cook and all sorts of things to stress over. On a similar note, do you want to come over to my apartment for dinner on Wednesday? David and Caroline already said they'll be there."

She shook her head. "Absolutely not. That's my LSAT score release day. Wednesday is reserved for crying."

"No, Wednesday is reserved for celebrating! That's why I'm cooking dinner. What's your favorite meal?" he asked.

She sighed. "Fine, if I score above a 170, I'll come to dinner."

He handed her the leftover pizza to stash in the fridge. "You can still get into a good law school without a 170."

"I don't just want a good school; I want a great school. Like Stanford or Harvard or Yale"—Evelyn argued—"and I need a near-perfect score for them to even consider my application. I'll come to dinner to celebrate if I get a 170."

"You studied every day for months," Liam reminded her. "I'm sure you did great, Evelyn."

She shrugged. "We'll find out."

"Liam, thanks for the party!" Oliver said as he waved goodbye and headed out the door.

"Bye Oliver!" Evelyn shouted.

"I should probably head out soon too," Liam said. "I have an early meeting at work tomorrow about some audits."

"Audits? That sounds boring," Aaron said.

"It sounds more interesting than being a business major," Liam spat back.

Aaron laughed. "We'll see what you say when I'm a billionaire CEO one day."

Evelyn just rolled her eyes. "I'll see you idiots next week." She grabbed her backpack and headed home.

Monday, September 9

Erica:

Do you want to meet for lunch?

After book club? At the cafeteria?

Or maybe that burger place you and Caroline like?

Oh wait no you're probably eating that for dinner

What about the pizza buffet instead?

Did you read the first chapter for book club today? It's great

I'm bringing cookies to book club

Nevermind... I think I burned them

How long are you supposed to bake cookies for?

Evelyn woke up to a barrage of texts from her honorary little sister. She had hoped her erratic sleep schedule wouldn't be a trait Erica learned from her, but the timestamps of the messages suggested Erica had already picked up the bad habit.

Evelyn:

> Depends on the recipe. Next time just buy some refrigerated cookie dough and read the back of the box. It'll tell you.

> We can get lunch at the cafeteria. The food isn't great but you should use your meal plan your mom pays for. Your wallet will thank you later.

Evelyn walked into the library before book club, wandering the second floor—Erica's favorite study spot—until she found the young girl staring at her laptop screen in the corner, eyes half closed.

"I brought you a gift." She handed her a cup.

"...coffee? I've never had coffee before." Erica looked at the cup like it was a foreign object from another planet.

"This is more like pure sugar with a splash of coffee in it. I think you'll like it," Evelyn said.

Erica took a small sip, then another. "Okay, Evelyn, I see why you like this so much." She set the cup down and closed her laptop.

Evelyn helped Erica pack up her computer and notebooks, and they headed back to the first floor of the library together.

Beckett was already setting up chairs in a circle. He waved at the girls as they walked in. "Hey, Erica! Did you like the first chapter of the book?"

"It was great," Erica said. "The world-building is amazing, and I love the way the author describes the scenery—it's beautiful."

"I really liked the dynamics between the three main characters," Beckett said. He set out the last chair and sat down. Erica sat beside him.

The book club members trickled in slowly. The discussion started on topic, talking about the introduction of the world and characters in the first chapter, but as many good discussions do, the conversation started a debate.

"I think fantasy can be overrated. It relies too much on magic and prophecies and 'chosen one' tropes to make the book interesting instead of having a complex plot with three-dimensional characters," Hannah said. She was the eldest member of the book club—a graduate student—and the only remaining founding member. "That's why I prefer realistic fiction or biographies or memoirs."

"But the real world is boring," Milo said.

"The real world isn't boring; we're just so caught up in what could be that we fail to notice the fascinating parts of what is," Hannah argued.

"But I like the escapism of it," Erica said. "Fantasy is great at distracting us from this world and allowing us to focus on another."

Hannah shrugged. "You're not wrong. I just think we spend too much time trying to escape reality and not enough time enjoying it."

Milo rolled his eyes. "I thought this was a book club, not a philosophy class."

"Sometimes, they're basically the same thing," Beckett said, before redirecting the conversation back to the original topic. "What did you think of the three main characters? Which one is your favorite?"

The discussion went smoothly from there until book club ended and everyone left the room. Erica and Evelyn stayed behind to help Beckett rearrange the chairs, then headed to the cafeteria for lunch.

The university cafeteria was a dreaded staple of freshman life. The small selection of mediocre food was bearable, but the repetition was the detrimental factor. Erica swiped her student ID at the front door, and they walked into the crowded space together.

"I haven't been here in a while," Evelyn said. She pointed to an isolated table in the corner. "That's where Aaron and I used to sit, back in the day."

"I'm surprised Liam didn't drag you to one of the large tables with all the extroverts," Erica said, filling a plate with chicken nuggets.

"Liam was a junior at the time; he didn't eat here. But he used to drag me and Aaron into hordes of extroverts in the student union all the time."

They sat down at the corner table, Evelyn taking her old seat and Erica taking Aaron's. It was painfully quiet at first. Erica stuffed her mouth with chicken nuggets, avoiding eye contact with Evelyn. Evelyn refused to break the silence. She knew Erica well, and the lunch invite could only mean one thing—Erica had something important on her mind, and Evelyn was willing to wait patiently and painfully until Erica finally spoke.

"So... when was the last time you went on a date?"

Evelyn almost choked on her drink. "Wait, what?"

"When was the last time you went on a date?"

Evelyn's mind started racing. She didn't mind answering the question, but why in the world would Erica be asking this? Since when did Erica care about Evelyn's relationship status? Erica didn't care about dating at all; she'd never been on a date herself and seemed to have no interest in doing so.

"Freshman year. So about 3 years ago," Evelyn finally answered.

"With who? Where did you go? What did you do? Was it fun?"

"His name was Alex. It was just dinner and a movie. I enjoyed it, but a week later he told me he didn't want to go on another date, so that was it."

"Well, that's... boring. I thought you'd have a more interesting story."

"It's typically not like the romance novels, Erica." Evelyn stole one of Erica's chicken nuggets, and the awkward silence resumed until Erica stood up to go get more food.

She came back a moment later, took a deep breath, and sat down across from Evelyn. "So... I have a date next week."

Evelyn almost choked on her drink a second time. "What? With who?"

"Beckett." She looked Evelyn in the eyes for the first time in the conversation, gauging her reaction carefully.

Evelyn hid her true emotions behind a neutral smile. Like an older sister, she felt an excitement to see Erica grow up and explore relationships mixed with a sudden urge to swaddle her in bubble wrap so that no one could harm her. Erica was so wise, yet so young and naive. Beckett seemed harmless, but so did the surface of the ocean on a calm, sunny day. Evelyn didn't know him well enough to judge his deeper motivations.

"Beckett?"

"Yes! He asked me on a date yesterday."

"Do you like him?" Evelyn asked, trying her best to keep her tone curious instead of cynical.

"Of course! He's really sweet, and I really like talking to him. He asked if we can get coffee at his favorite bookstore. Doesn't that sound like fun?" Erica was clearly ecstatic, and Evelyn didn't want to squash her joy.

"That sounds great. You'll have to tell me how it goes." *You'll have to tell me every single detail,* Evelyn thought. She wanted to know every place they went, every step he took, every single word of their conversation.

"Now I just need to figure out what to wear, what to talk about, and what coffee I'm supposed to buy," Erica said."Just wear whatever you feel like, talk about whatever you enjoy, and order whatever you want. There's no right or wrong here, Erica. It's a date. Just enjoy it."

Erica took a deep breath. "Okay. You're right. I'm sure it'll be great."

Tuesday, September 10

If Wednesday was reserved for crying, then Tuesday was reserved for overthinking.

There were only 24 more hours until Evelyn's LSAT score was released. 23 hours. 22 hours. She counted down every second as she went about her normal Tuesday schedule—statistics study group, lunch, topology class, psychology class, dinner. She was like a sailor lost at sea, helplessly floating through the waves of her routine, too distracted by thoughts of life after her bachelor's degree to pay attention in her undergraduate classes.

If she could just make a 170, she could get into a top law school, then work at a top law firm. Of course there were other schools, less prestigious schools, but those weren't what she wanted. Those weren't the schools she had worked so hard for. What would she do if her score was too low for her dream school? What if her score was too low for any law school?

What else could she do with a math degree? She could teach, but it sounded emotionally draining to handle a classroom full of high schoolers—or worse, middle schoolers. She could become a paralegal, but what would it be like to work for a bunch of lawyers when she desperately wished to be one herself? Maybe she could study even more and take the LSAT again, but it would probably delay her start date by a year, and what would she do in the meantime?

Maybe she could travel the world and go off the grid. Somewhere colder sounded nice. Maybe Antarctica. The penguins wouldn't care about her LSAT score. Her thoughts spiraled like a tornado gaining momentum. She tried to sleep that night, but couldn't, until her exhaustion outweighed her insomnia, and finally, her thoughts turned into dreams.

Wednesday, September 11

The LSAT scores were always released at precisely 9 a.m. Unfortunately, Evelyn's 8:30 a.m. professor didn't care.

She dragged herself to her early morning class and sat in the back with her laptop open. She copied down the professor's work in her notebook with her right hand and incessantly refreshed the website with her left. Her phone vibrated in her pocket, but she ignored it. It wasn't important in the grand scheme of the moment.

Finally, at 9 a.m., the test score appeared. She dropped her pencil and stared at the score, her mind racing like a derailed supersonic train.

166.

It was a good score, but not good enough. She had passed the test in a sense, but she had failed herself. All those months of studying felt wasted now, her entire summer of work thrown out the window. This one little number on her screen prophesied her entire future, and she didn't like what it told.

Just yesterday, Stanford, Harvard, Yale, and the other top law schools were open doors of opportunity. Today, she watched those doors slam closed in an instant.

This wasn't what she wanted. A tear streaked down her face, but she quickly wiped it away. She couldn't react to the sudden disappointment. She was still in a classroom of oblivious students quietly scribbling down equations just like any other day.

She picked back up her pencil, trying to copy down the work on the whiteboard and catch up with what she missed. Her hand shook nervously, frustrating her, which only made her hand shake more. She already dreaded the time it would take to decipher the illegible notes later.

It wasn't until after class that she remembered the vibrating of her phone.

Liam:

dinner tonight?

She sighed at the message. She wrote, deleted, and rewrote the reply multiple times until she settled on a response.

Evelyn:

Can I break the 170 score rule?

She received a reply almost immediately.

Liam:

let me ask the rule maker.

hey evelyn, can evelyn break the 170 rule you made?

Her laughter interrupted her tears, even if only for a second.

Evelyn:

Sure, I guess I'll allow it.

Liam:

> *then i'll see you at 7.*

The day was a blur.

Evelyn studied in the library with her psychology classmates, attended office hours for help with a difficult topology problem, and completed homework assignments in the honors lounge. Her rigid schedule allowed for her passiveness, like a GPS guiding her to her destination with little effort. She didn't need to make decisions or think of the future; she could simply complete the task scheduled for the given moment, floating wherever the waves of her calendar took her. Tomorrow, maybe, she could plan for the future, try to fight the riptide and make her way back to shore, but today, she only had enough energy to keep herself from drowning.

Evelyn drove to Liam's apartment, blaring pop music on the radio in a poor attempt to drown out her sadness. She parked in front of the building and walked up to his apartment, number 1128. She double checked the number on the door with the address on her phone, despite visiting multiple times before, and knocked twice.

Liam peeked out the door with a gentle smile. "Hey, Evelyn. How are you?" he asked. She shrugged quietly, staring at her feet. "Come inside," Liam said, opening the door farther.

She walked past him into the small apartment. Caroline and David lounged on a worn-down blue couch in the living room. Aaron sat on the rug, losing in a video game to Oliver. He hit pause when he noticed Evelyn walk in.

"Evelyn! You made it!" Aaron said. "Come on, sit down. Dinner is almost ready."

Evelyn pulled Liam's desk chair over to the makeshift living room of the studio apartment. "What game are you playing?" she asked, glancing at the TV screen. "Is that a golf game? That's... interesting."

"Boring," Caroline corrected. "You can call it boring."

"It's not boring; it's fun. Especially when I'm winning," Oliver said.

Liam distributed bowls to the group, handing the first one to Evelyn. "Chicken tortilla soup. Careful, it's hot."

"That's my favorite," Evelyn said with a smile. She tasted the soup cautiously, trying not to burn her tongue. "This tastes like my childhood."

"It should. We stole the recipe from your mom," Oliver said.

"Wait, what?" Evelyn looked around the group confused, quickly realizing that everyone else already knew the origins of the recipe.

"Well, the other day, Liam asked what you wanted for dinner today, and you didn't answer, so I texted your mom and asked what your favorite meal was. She sent me the recipe," Caroline said.

"I gave you my mom's number in case of emergencies!" Evelyn argued with a grin on her face.

"You had a rough day, princess. This was an emergency," Oliver said.

Evelyn looked back at Liam, who was still distributing soup. "You told them about my test score, didn't you?"

He nodded. "They were going to find out eventually, and I didn't want them to drive you crazy asking about it all day. You don't have to talk about it right now if you don't want to."

Evelyn started to cry. She couldn't hold back the flood of emotions anymore.

Caroline walked over and hugged her. "It's okay, Evelyn, it's okay."

She took a deep breath. "How about we just eat soup and play that fighting game I'm bad at?"

Aaron handed her a controller. "We can do that."

According to the game developers, the characters in the fighting games were balanced, meaning anyone could win with any character. Evelyn wasn't convinced. Her character Rose Thorn lost every single round to Oliver's character

Thunder Bolt, and it wasn't even a close fight. By the end of most rounds, she had zero lives left while he still had all three. He tried to show her some tips; apparently, she needed to "memorize the combos" and "play more defensively" and "practice with her main more often". She barely understood what she was doing; she used the left joystick to move, the X to jump, and the Y to punch, but there were ten other buttons with functions unknown to her. According to Oliver, Rose Thorn had other powers, like restraining the opponent with vines or throwing poisonous flowers, but Evelyn could barely understand the three mechanics she already knew. Maybe that's why she lost every game. Thunder Bolt killed Rose Thorn over and over, but she never truly died. She was always back again, ready to start another round with another sassy insult.

"Okay, Oliver, this is just cruel," David said as Oliver won again. He picked up a controller and added himself to Evelyn's team. "I'll help."

"Two versus one isn't fair," Aaron said. He turned on another controller to join Oliver's team.

"Wait, I don't want to be left out," Caroline argued, joining Evelyn and David's group.

All eyes expectantly fell on Liam as he put away the last dish. He sighed. "I guess someone needs to even out the teams."

The group cheered as he sat down and joined them. They connected the controllers, picked their characters, and started the game.

David ran straight for Oliver, determined to end his winning streak. Aaron dueled Caroline and quickly lost. Liam, in an effort to avenge his teammate, fought and defeated Caroline.

Evelyn had a different strategy. As soon as the round started, Rose Thorn ran. She didn't need to parry attacks if no one was in range to hit her. She decided her best defense was to stand far away from the offense.

After a long, hard fight, David beat Oliver. He tried to help his girlfriend beat Liam, but it was too late. Caroline was out of the game. Instead, he went for revenge, trying to swing at Liam but quickly getting thrown off the map, leaving only Liam and Evelyn to battle.

Liam looked at Evelyn from across the living room. "Are you going to come fight?"

"I like hiding in the corner of the screen," Evelyn argued.

He stood up and walked to her. "Want me to show you a combo?" He pointed to the buttons on her controller to show her how to perform the moves. It was confusing at first, with multiple inputs required in an arbitrary order, but after trying it a few times, her hands learned the pattern. Liam picked back up his controller and moved his character to hers. She executed the combo, and his character flew backwards several feet. She smiled. "Do I win now?"

"You can certainly try," Liam said.

She managed to hit the combo again, but ultimately still lost. She felt accomplished nonetheless.

"We need a rematch. That was just a warmup," Caroline insisted, starting another round.

They played the game late into the night. For Evelyn, the day had been reserved for crying, but for Rose Thorn, the day had been reserved for competing. The beauty of a fighting game was that every loss was temporary. Every few minutes, Rose Thorn was revived as if the last fight didn't even happen. There were constant resets and infinite attempts.

Unfortunately, Evelyn didn't live in a fighting game. The events of today would inevitably affect the events of tomorrow.

Thursday, September 12

Despite the lack of classes, Evelyn's morning was busy. Her to-do list was filled with other obnoxious tasks she needed to get out of the way, like laundry and dishes and grocery shopping.

She drove to the store and returned with several bags full of frozen meals and cans of soup. As she was carefully organizing the food in their pantry, Bethany returned from class. She tossed her backpack on the counter with a sigh then grabbed a box of cookies from the pantry and crashed onto the couch.

"What's wrong?" Evelyn asked.

"I didn't say anything was wrong," Bethany snapped back.

"You didn't have to. What's wrong?"

Bethany stuffed a cookie in her mouth. "Calculus." The word was barely recognizable through her mouthful of food.

"Do you want my help?" Evelyn asked.

"I want a nap and to drop out of school."

"Let me rephrase: do you need my help? You'll have to do the assignments eventually."

"...fine." She pulled her homework and notes out of her backpack and set them on the coffee table.

Evelyn sat on the couch with Bethany and talked her through the questions. The professor had filled this assignment with particularly tricky problems, so it was no surprise Bethany was confused. After half an hour of work, they had figured out a few of the answers.

"You just need to use integration by parts until part of the expression matches the integral you started with. Then you can set the starting integral equal to the new expression and solve with algebra, just like solving for x." Evelyn wrote out an example as she explained the process.

"How do you know all of this? It comes so naturally to you," Bethany said.

Evelyn laughed. "I've studied this for four years. It didn't always come so easily."

"I think you're just a genius. You'll probably end up at Harvard or something."

She sighed. "I wish." She wandered into her bedroom and habitually opened her laptop.

Her LSAT score displayed on the screen. 166. Unfortunately, it hadn't miraculously changed overnight. She closed the tab on her laptop, but she couldn't close the tab in her brain. The image of the score was burned into her memories, like a scar that would fade but never quite disappear.

Saturday, September 14

The desk at Evelyn's part-time job was full of small knick-knacks and pictures of someone else's kids. The main receptionist worked Monday through Friday, and Evelyn was simply a Saturday substitute.

The managing partner, Mr. Alfred, waved at her as he passed the front desk. She was surprised to see him here this early on a Saturday. His schedule was erratic and busy. She had asked him about it once, and he simply responded that he was "always in the office when needed."

She answered the phone and gave clients directions to conference rooms. Between tasks, she worked on cleaning the desk. The receptionist had left it a mess; Friday must have been a busy day. She placed the pens in their cup, the sticky notes in their drawer, and the books on the small shelf. The last few books in the row were Evelyn's LSAT study books. The lawyers had encouraged her to spend some time in the office studying for her tests. It was a nice method of staying productive when the phone wasn't ringing and the lobby was empty.

She debated on taking the books home, but there was no point. Her test was finished. She could leave them for another future student to torture themselves with.

Mr. Alfred left the office at the same time as Evelyn. He held the elevator for her, and she stepped inside. "Hey, Ms. Evelyn. How is the semester going?"

Ms. Evelyn. He always called her that, as if Evelyn was her last name, as if she was his boss and not his employee.

"It's going well. I'm keeping my grades up. Partial differential equations is hard, but the rest isn't too difficult."

"Are you still on track to graduate by May?"

She nodded. "Yes, sir."

He smiled. "Good. We're going to miss you when you leave us for school. You have a lot of potential, Ms. Evelyn."

"Thank you, sir."

The elevator dinged, and the doors opened, marking the end of their conversation. Evelyn fidgeted with her pen as she watched Mr. Alfred leave. She appreciated his encouragement, but she despised his confidence in her. It set an expectation that her LSAT score would never allow her to meet.

Evelyn sat in her dorm room, staring at her laptop screen. She had reopened the LSAT score page, as if she could forget the three digits that determined her entire future.

She took out her phone and dialed her mom's number. She had to share her score with her mom eventually. She might as well do it now.

The phone rang for a second before her mom answered, giddy as always.

"Hi, honey! How are you? How's your day going?"

Evelyn leaned back in her chair. "Hey, Mom. I'm doing ok."

"That's good to hear. I miss you so much! Avery misses you too."

"Is she at school right now?" Evelyn asked.

"I hope so," her mom said, her cheerfulness stained by a tinge of frustration. "I told her she couldn't keep skipping class, but you know her. She cares a lot more about her social life than her academics. At least she has good friends. They just get ice cream at Scoops when they skip class. They stay out of trouble for the most part."

"That's good. I'll try to convince her to go to class."

"Can you help her pass geometry too? She's making a C, but I know she can do better. How are your grades? How's school? You're not skipping class, right?"

"I'm not skipping class, I promise. I... I got my LSAT score."

"What did you get?" Her mom asked the question as if Evelyn said she won the lottery. Of course she would assume Evelyn's score was good; she had always been the optimist of the family.

"166."

"That's amazing! I'm so proud of you! I knew you'd do gr—"

"It's not great, Mom. It's not enough to get into Harvard."

"It's a good score, Evie. You don't have to go to Harvard or Yale or Stanford to be a wonderful lawyer. Isn't there a law school near the college you're at now?"

"Yes, but no one has heard of it. I can't get a job at one of the best law firms unless I go to one of the best schools."

"You know, you're one of the best students. It doesn't matter what school you go to."

"It does matter, Mom!" Tears streaked down Evelyn's face. She caught a glimpse of herself in the mirror. She wasn't cute when she cried like the love interests in movies. Her eyes were swollen and her vision obscured. Her tears mixed with her mascara, covering her face in dark lines. "It's all that matters. It's all I've worked for. I worked so hard in high school to get into this college, to get into the honors program, to get financial aid. There were hours and hours of SAT prep, ACT prep, scholarship applications, keeping my grades up."

"Honey, take a deep breath." Her mom tried to interrupt, but Evelyn was too absorbed in her rant to hear.

"Then I come to college and do the same thing again. There's so many tests, so many assignments, so many late nights of little to no sleep, all to get into law school. And then I get a summer break, but it's not really a break, because I need an internship for my resume. I get a full-time internship, eight hours a day, and on top of that,

I spend hours and hours studying for this stupid test, all to get a score that's still not good enough. I tried my best, and it still wasn't good enough. I'm not good enough." With a ragged breath, she collapsed into her chair.

"Evelyn, if that's your standard, then no one is good enough," her mom said calmly. The cheerfulness had left her voice now, but she still spoke with a sense of peace.

"The people who make it into Harvard are good enough," Evelyn said, fidgeting with her hair.

"You said it yourself. You did everything you could. The rest is luck. Evelyn, do you remember playing Monopoly as a kid?"

"Of course. That game was miserable. Avery hated it; she always lost." Evelyn remembered long evenings in the living room, the floor filled with cards and colorful fake money. With so many pieces, there was barely room left to sit. It often took multiple nights to finish a game, but rarely did Avery's attention span last that long. She didn't enjoy playing the game, and Evelyn didn't like leaving it unfinished. They begged their mom for a new board game, but there wasn't much money to spare. Finally, for Christmas, they were given new games, and they never played Monopoly again.

"Avery always lost because she didn't know the strategies. But you and I? We mastered it. We knew exactly how to win, yet we never both won. Sometimes it was me, and sometimes it was you. Even if we both played perfectly, the dice had to roll in our favor. This is like that. Evelyn, you played the game perfectly. You did everything you could. Don't beat yourself up over a dice roll."

"But what if I had studied more? Just another few hours. Maybe it would have been different."

"Maybe so, or maybe not. Unless you studied twenty-four hours a day, you always could have studied more. Maybe if you studied more, you would have been so tired that you didn't even remember what you studied, and then you'd be asking if you should have studied less. There's infinitely many 'what-ifs', and you don't have infinite time to analyze each one."

Evelyn took a deep breath. "You're right, Mom."

"I know. I love you, okay? Keep me updated. I miss you."

"I miss you too. Have a good day."

She hung up the phone and looked at her computer.

166.

She hit the refresh button.

166. It didn't change. This one little number, some ones and zeros in a computer somewhere, threw a wrench in her entire future. It burned her entire plan to the ground.

Or maybe not. She could still apply to Harvard. Was it worth a try? It was probably a waste of time. If she didn't try, however, it would simply bring more 'what-ifs'. Applying for Harvard, Stanford, and Yale would be inviting rejection, but maybe rejection would be better than the unknown.

To-Do List: Sept. 15–21

- [ ] Read Chapter 3 for book club
- [ ] Ask Erica about her date
- [ ] Partial Differential Equations homework
- [ ] Partial Differential Equations quiz
- [ ] Buy snacks for stats study group
- [ ] Study for stats test
- [ ] Stats homework
- [ ] Psychology discussion board
- [ ] Read psychology textbook chapters 11 & 12
- [ ] Start psychology project
- [ ] Topology homework
- [ ] Read topology textbook chapter 5
- [ ] Take machine learning quiz
- [ ] Research for AI essay
- [ ] Buy more paper for printer
- [ ] Meet with advisor for graduation audit
- [ ] Wash towels
- [ ] Apply for law school

3

Sunday, September 15

"How are the law school applications going?" Oliver asked as Evelyn walked into David's house.

"I haven't started yet."

"Procrastinating won't make it easier," he said.

"I know that, okay? Leave me alone," Evelyn snapped back at him.

"I'm sorry. I'm just trying to help," Oliver said. Aaron placed a hand on her shoulder.

"I know. Sorry." She dumped out her bag of dice onto the table. "Real life is exhausting. Let's just play the game."

The party left the inn the next morning on a mission to meet Kinsley. Finding her house was easy. She lived with her parents uptown in a castle-like mansion that was anything but subtle.

They watched the home from afar. Several guards circled the perimeter, and Clarissa assumed there were more guards hidden.

"It's going to be hard to sneak in there," Jemma said.

"Or, Jemma, we could try being civil for once. We're returning Kinsley's prized possession. I'm sure she'll let us in if we just ask nicely," Elijah said.

While the others studied the guard patterns, Clarissa looked at the home itself. There were several tall towers that probably gave a beautiful view of the city (and good visibility to watch for incoming trouble). The building was surrounded by beautiful landscaping. The perfectly curated garden was full of colorful flowers and bushes, including many plants Clarissa had never seen before. Large trees shaded a walking path from the house to a small gazebo surrounded by an orchard of ripe fruit trees. A young lady—probably employed by the house, since the guards didn't mind her—filled a basket with oranges from the trees. She wore a silky lavender dress, simple but beautiful. The guards, likewise, were dressed in expensive clothing: matching blue uniforms with leather belts and shoes.

Clarissa glanced down at her tattered and stained clothes and touched her matted hair that hadn't been washed in a week. "There's no way they're letting us in."

"We could go shopping!" Jemma said. "We just need to make ourselves not look homeless, and then maybe the guards will talk to us."

Elijah rolled his eyes. "We don't have the money for makeovers."

Jemma smirked. "There are plenty of ways to get new things without money."

"Most of those involve us getting arrested," Jareth said

"Only if we get caught," Jemma countered.

"Even if you disguise us as rich kids, we still look like a threat. We have too many weapons, and I don't feel safe leaving them behind," Derek said.

"I have another idea, but you won't like it," Jareth told Elijah.

Elijah narrowed his eyes. "What?"

"We send Clarissa in alone."

"Absolutely not." Elijah quickly dismissed the idea.

"It could work. She's good at talking to people, and she'd fit in with high society better than the rest of us. We want the Lister family to actually like us. They could be a valuable ally in the future," Jareth argued.

Eli glared at Jareth, and Jareth just stared back in silence. Jareth tilted his head, and Eli rolled his eyes again.

"They're talking in their heads again, aren't they?" Jemma whispered to Clarissa.

She nodded. "It's a useful spell."

"Why can't we just cast it to Kinsley?" Derek asked.

"The spell doesn't work that way."

"It's magic. Can't you just make it work that way?" Jemma asked.

"Just because I know a little magic doesn't mean I can bend reality to my will. I can only cast the message spell on people I've met or people I can see."

"That's stupid," Jemma replied. They watched Jareth and Eli, seeing only the body language of the telepathic conversation. Neither of the boys seemed happy. Eli closed his eyes and took a deep breath. Clarissa noticed Jareth ever-so-slightly grin.

"Let's go back to the inn," Elijah said. "We'll discuss the plan there." He led them through the town. Jareth subtly insisted on walking in the back of the group. Whether it was to keep an eye on them or get far away from Eli, Clarissa wasn't sure. All she knew was that she didn't appreciate being kept in the dark.

'What's going on?' She messaged Jareth telepathically, secretly.

'Eli didn't want you going in alone. He's worried you'll get hurt,' Jareth replied.

'Did you convince him it's the best idea?'

'Actually, we came up with a better one.'

They walked into the inn and sat down. "Alright, time for the important questions," Derek said. "What's the plan, and does it involve an underground fighting ring?"

"The plan requires talking to people, not fighting them," Jareth said.

"That's a boring plan," Derek argued.

"It doesn't involve you anyways," Elijah said. "Clarissa and Jareth will go inside and try to talk with Kinsley. Everyone else needs to stay away from the mansion; we don't want security to see us. If this plan fails, Jareth can disguise himself with magic, and Clarissa can sit out so we're all unknown faces to the guards. Understood?"

"What do we do in the meantime?" Jemma asked.

"Go with Derek to an underground fighting ring. I couldn't care less." Eli stood up from the table and glared at Jareth. "Be back before sunset. Stay safe."

"You know I will," Jareth said to Eli, who nodded and walked off.

"Well, that was tense. Let's go explore the city!" Jemma jumped to her feet and grabbed Derek's arm to pull him along with her. Clarissa laughed at the small girl trying to move a guy twice her height. He didn't budge, watching Jemma struggle in amusement, until finally he gave in and followed her out the door.

"So how do we get in?" Clarissa asked Jareth.

"I thought you'd have an idea," Jareth countered.

"I have many. We can't just tell them we're hired adventurers; they'll think we're assassins. I could pretend to be a friend of Kinsley's and hope they'll let us talk to her, but they'll send me in alone. You need a story."

"I could be your bodyguard."

Clarissa shook her head. "That's too intimidating. We need to seem harmless. I want them to think we're not remotely capable of hurting someone." She paused for a second, twiddling with her hair. A silent smile spread across her face. "Do you think you could pretend to be my boyfriend?"

Jareth grinned. "Are you doubting my acting skills?"

"I'm doubting your flirting skills."

"Claire, sweetheart, don't doubt me." He took her hand in his and gently lifted it to his lips.

She smiled. "I'm not quite yet convinced." She stood from the table and intertwined her fingers in his. "Luckily, you have an entire shopping trip to prove your skills."

Jareth was a much better liar than Clarissa anticipated. He took the lead in the tailor shop. "I'm Jareth, and this is my girlfriend Clarissa. We're travelers from the west. It took us weeks to get here, and we had an unfortunate encounter with some wolves." He looked down at his battered clothes. "We're in need of new outfits. We're a little short on gold at the moment, but I promised my dear Claire we'd come see the best dresses in the city." He smiled at Clarissa and wrapped an arm around her. "We asked some locals, and they sent us here. Do you think you can help us out?"

The man nodded eagerly. "Of course!" He walked off to check the store's inventory in the back, almost skipping with joy, while his wife began taking Clarissa's measurements.

The store was made up of a single room divided by tattered curtains. Paint was chipping off the splintered walls, and the floors creaked with every step. Considering the location in the impoverished sector of town, one that tourists tended to avoid, the couple likely didn't see new customers often. For this exact reason, it was the perfect place for the fake couple to visit. Clarissa desperately hoped the excitement of newcomers would help them ignore the dirt that covered her and overlook any holes in the story of her arrival.

"What color are you looking for?" the woman asked Clarissa. "I think you would look good in a dark green. No, wait, maybe it should be emerald to match your eyes."

Clarissa smiled. "You're the expert. I trust your judgment."

The woman shouted some numbers to her husband in the other room, then moved on to measure Jareth. Her husband returned with an emerald green dress and a cream-colored corset top. "Go try this on in the back room."

She did as he instructed. The silky green dress reached all the way to her ankles. The fabric was light and flowy, making it easy to move and walk (and fight). The corset top was a necessary evil, but its beauty made Clarissa question her hatred for corsets. Embroidered yellow flowers and green foliage accented the cream fabric, perfectly matching the dress.

She walked back into the main room. Jareth smiled. "You look beautiful, love." He took her hand and twirled her around, the skirt of her dress weightlessly floating around her.

"You're next, young man," the woman told Jareth. She handed him a stack of black and cream clothing. He walked away to change.

"What's your name?" Clarissa asked the woman.

"Oh, I didn't introduce myself earlier! My name is Aria," she said.

"It's nice to meet you, Aria. I love your little shop. I'm so glad Jareth found this place."

"You and your boyfriend are absolutely adorable," Aria grinned. "I can tell he really loves you."

"He really does," Clarissa said.

"Do you think he'll propose soon?" the woman whispered.

Clarissa smiled, blushing a little. "I sure hope so. At least now I'll have a beautiful dress to wear the day he does."

"You know, I make wedding dresses too," the woman said with a wink.

Clarissa grinned. This was her area of expertise: building a believable story and flawlessly acting the part. She had only been in the shop for half an hour, but the woman adored Clarissa, just like Clarissa wanted.

Jareth returned with his own set of new clothes: black pants, a cream-colored shirt, and a long gray cloak. Clarissa held both his hands between them. "You look great."

"You both do," Aria said. "Now stop moving. Let me finish with the pins."

After another half hour of fitting, she dismissed them. "Now, you said you need these outfits today, correct?"

Clarissa nodded. "Can we come back in a couple hours to pick them up?"

"Sure. For the clothes and expedited alterations, it would normally be 120 gold, but I could knock it down to 100 for you."

"Could we do 80? We're really short on coins here," Jareth said.

She didn't seem convinced, but Clarissa took a step towards her and whispered in her ear. "I'll come back here for my wedding dress soon. Please?"

Aria couldn't help but smile. "Okay, fine. 80 gold."

They paid half as a deposit and left, wandering the streets of the city to pass the time.

"Did you know you're going to propose soon?" Clarissa said.

"I am?" Jareth asked with wide eyes.

"You are, and Aria is going to make my wedding dress."

Jareth laughed. "You really have a way with people," he said as he gently wrapped his arm around her. "We need some more fake-dating practice. Let's go find a jewelry store."

"And we'll end the game there for the night," David said.

"We still don't get to meet Kinsley?!" Caroline complained again.

David shrugged. "Maybc next week."

As per usual, they packed up their dice and leftover pizza. "Did you ever get your PDEs test score back?" Liam asked Evelyn.

"I never even checked my grade!" She had been so preoccupied by her LSAT score that it had completely slipped her mind. She opened her grades on her phone and painstakingly watched the loading icon spin. Liam came to watch over her shoulder right as the grade popped up: 97.

"I told you so," Liam said with a grin. "I knew you'd ace it."

Evelyn rolled her eyes. "You were right." She was grateful for the grade, but it didn't matter. Law schools would throw out her application based on her LSAT score before they even looked at her math grades, and if she didn't go to law school, most jobs would only ever look at her GPA anyways. What was the point in studying 40 hours for a number on a page no one would ever see?

Liam placed a hand on her shoulder. "Don't be so hard on yourself."

"What do you mean?" Evelyn asked.

"It doesn't take telepathy to know you're overthinking. I can see it in your eyes."

Liam's comment about overthinking became the new subject of Evelyn's overthinking. She walked into her bedroom, tossed her backpack into the corner, and crashed into her bed. How could he read her mind like that? It didn't make any sense.

She curled up under her fuzzy blanket and closed her exposing green eyes, trying her best to quiet her mind, but her thoughts hit her from all directions like snow in a swirling blizzard. How could he see through her skull and get a glimpse of the script being read in her brain? More importantly, why couldn't she peer into his mind in the same way? It made her question her sanity and social skills. Clarissa, she realized, wouldn't have this problem. She knew the thoughts and intentions of everyone she met. Evelyn, on the other hand, was clueless, a little frustrated, and extremely tired. Her consciousness slipped away, replaced by vivid dreams of worlds that made more sense than her own.

Monday, September 16

This week, Evelyn didn't wake up to a mountain of text messages from Erica. Instead, they came during class.

Erica:

> *Hey Evelyn I have my date tonight*

I need your help!

What am I supposed to wear???

I'll send you some options

The other eight text messages were pictures of Erica posed in front of her mirror in different outfits. The first was a long, midnight-blue dress covered in silver accents and rhinestones. Evelyn suspected it was from her high school prom. The second was a gray blazer over a white shirt, paired with black pants, reminding Evelyn of the outfit she wore to her internship interview. The other options included an oversized sweater with leggings and boots (which was too hot for the September weather, but Erica insisted she "looked cute in winter clothes"), and jean shorts with a baseball jersey and cap from her favorite team. In the last photo, she was wearing a short, overly revealing red dress that would easily spark outrage in her parents.

Evelyn:

You look cute in everything :) but don't stress over clothes.

She thought about reminding Erica that the date was at a coffee shop and not a costume party, but the more words she typed, the more opportunities Erica had to misunderstand.

Evelyn:

Find your favorite pair of jeans and cute shirt.

Erica:

That's a genius idea!

Erica showed up to book club wearing ripped jeans, a lavender shirt, and spotless white sneakers, already prepared for her date that night after class. She sat in the chair next to Evelyn.

The students at book club debated whether world-building was too high of a priority over character building in the fantasy genre. Evelyn, however, heard little of the conversation after the initial question. She was too focused on Erica, who was too focused on the boy. Her eyes watched him like a moth watches a flame. She absorbed every word he said and laughed at every poor attempt at a joke.

Beckett's affection was less obvious but indisputably present. Every few minutes, his eyes drifted from the speaker in the group to Erica, but the moment she glanced at him, his eyes darted away. Every time she spoke, his face lit up, and he leaned forward to listen, absorbing every word she said.

It was classic young love. They hadn't even been on a date, yet they were already obsessed with each other.

As book club ended and students scattered, Erica pulled Evelyn aside. "I'm a little nervous."

"You look a little more than nervous," Evelyn commented.

"Okay, I'm absolutely terrified! What if everything goes wrong and he hates me?"

Evelyn placed her hands on Erica's shoulders. "If he hates you, he's an idiot."

"I'm freaking out, Evelyn! I have absolutely no clue what I'm doing! What if everything goes wrong?"

Evelyn shrugged. "Then I'll punch him."

Erica paused. "When have you punched people before? Do you even know how to throw a punch?"

"No. But if he's mean to you, I'm sure I can figure it out. I'm sure your older brother could help me too."

Erica broke eye contact, looking at the ground.

"You didn't tell Rowan you're going on a date," Evelyn guessed. Erica's face confirmed Evelyn's theory.

"He's too overprotective," Erica argued. Evelyn sighed. She'd only met Rowan a few times, but she knew he genuinely loved his little sister. It was true that he was watchful of Erica's well-being, but he was far from overbearing.

"He just cares about you, Erica. Keeping secrets from him isn't a good idea. I'm guessing you didn't tell your mom either?"

"I'll tell them tonight after the date, I promise!"

Evelyn gave Erica a hug. "You can tell them tonight. For now, focus on the date and the conversations."

"I'll just drown all my nerves in an extra large vanilla cold brew," Erica said.

"Maybe you should go for something other than coffee," Evelyn recommended.

"Peppermint hot chocolate?" Erica asked.

Evelyn nodded. "That's a great choice." The last thing the young girl needed to add to her jittery nerves was an overdose of caffeine. "Go to your chemistry lecture, and text me after the date. Remember, you can always text me if anything goes wrong. I'll come up with a good excuse for you to leave."

Erica hugged her again before running off to class.

Evelyn grabbed a sandwich and an energy drink in the student union before her next back-to-back classes. It took a lot of conscious effort to stay awake during the three hours of lecturing, but between the caffeine and four pages of bad sketches, she somehow managed.

She checked her phone when she left class, and again her screen was filled with notifications.

Caroline:

Who wants to play board games tonight?

Aaron:

I'm in!

Liam:

sounds like fun. i have a new strategy game i can bring.

Oliver:

i can pick up food on the way, any objections to chicken strips?

Aaron:

What kind of crazy person would object to chicken strips?

Caroline:

Cool! David's house at 6pm :)

David:

I'm not sure when my house became the default meeting place

Aaron:

That's your punishment for having actual money and buying an actual house, unlike the rest of us.

David:

Fair enough

Oliver:

> *liam you better not bring another hour long strategy game that hurts my brain. if it makes me do math it's not a good game*

Liam:

> *i make no promises. evelyn, are you coming?*

Aaron:

> *Evelyn!!! Come play board games!!!*

Liam:

> *I need you to come so you can vote for my strategy game.*

Aaron:

> *Or you can come vote AGAINST his strategy game and watch the chaos unfold*

Oliver:

> *vote against the strategy game to keep us sane*

Caroline:

> *Guys chill she's probably in class, she'll text us back afterwards*

Aaron:

> *:(*

Evelyn read through the texts as she walked to the honors lounge, sipping the last of her energy drink.

Evelyn:
I can't. I need to study for my stats test on Wednesday.

Aaron:
Games are more fun than studying.

Evelyn:
Don't you have a marketing test tomorrow?

Aaron:
Like I said, games are more fun than studying.

Liam:
good luck on your test evelyn!

Caroline:
How about board games part 2 on Wednesday?

Evelyn:
If I can finish some of my homework by then, sure.

She took a seat in her normal corner of the honors lounge, claiming a clean whiteboard to deface with statistical distributions. She pulled out her collection of colored dry-erase markers and started filling the blank space with every piece of information she might need for her test: distributions, properties, means, variances, and derivations. To most onlookers, the math looked like a jumbled foreign language, but to Evelyn, it was a masterpiece. She loved the way statistics interpreted a qualitative world in quantitative ways.

"What are you working on?" A voice interrupted her focus. She spun around to see Melanie watching her work.

"I have a statistics test in a couple of days." Evelyn turned back to the whiteboard to refocus.

"That sounds hard. Good luck." Melanie sat down at her own table.

Evelyn sighed. It was undoubtedly, exhaustingly, dreadfully hard. It was beautiful, but it was torture.

She finished her notes on the whiteboard after a few hours and moved on to her previously graded homework assignments. With the answers covered, she worked on solving each problem. Hopefully, if she could solve the homework problems, the test would be easy, but there were never any guarantees.

She walked home as the sun set. Erica kept her promise and sent updates about her date with Beckett.

Erica:

The date was so much fun!

We talked a lot. We have so much in common

We were there for like two hours

> *And he told me he liked my shirt! He thought it was cute :)*

> *You give good fashion advice for someone who only wears sweatpants and t-shirts*

> *Oh and he bought me hot chocolate! And a new book! No one told me you get free stuff on dates*

> *We have another date Sunday :) He wants to eat dinner and go bowling*

Evelyn was glad Erica's date went well, but she struggled to focus on that bit of joy. Her thoughts wandered to the quizzes she needed to take that night and the homeworks she knew she would fail to finish. She dreaded tomorrow's exhaustion, given how little sleep she was going to get.

It wasn't until midnight that she realized she'd forgotten to eat dinner.

Wednesday, September 18

Evelyn had three simple goals for the day: ace her statistics test, finish as much homework as possible, and save a little energy for board game night. She was well aware that she would probably need to sacrifice the last one to accomplish the first two. The test wasn't until 3:30 p.m., which meant she had sufficient time to study and excess time to stress.

After her morning class, she returned to the honors lounge, where her statistics test review drawn on the whiteboard the night before had already been replaced with a list of biology terms and unrelated drawings of frogs.

She erased the frogs and started on her topology homework, filling the whiteboard with a dictionary of vocabulary words: metric space, homeomorphism, manifold. Even words like 'closed' and 'open' and 'neighborhood' were redefined in the new language.

"More statistics?" Melanie watched curiously.

"Worse. Topology," Evelyn responded.

"Sit down," Melanie demanded. She grabbed a chair at the nearest table.

"I'm kind of busy," Evelyn argued, continuing her work.

"No, we need to talk. Sit down," Melanie demanded again.

Evelyn glanced back at her. Melanie stared her down until, finally, Evelyn took a seat. "It's about Erica," Melanie explained, leaving Evelyn only more confused.

"Why?"

"Specifically, Erica and Beckett."

"Leave the two of them alone," Evelyn said. "I don't know what drama you're trying to start, but I don't want to be a part of it, and you'd better not drag my friend into it."

"I'm not trying to start drama! I'm trying to stop it. Beckett isn't who he says he is. He's a liar. He's manipulative. He'll date any girl he finds attractive until she dares to disagree with him, and then he'll break up with her and make sure everyone knows. It's absolutely toxic."

Her story sounded like a lesson learned only from experience. "How do you know this?" Evelyn asked.

Melanie sighed. "It's not important."

"It is," Evelyn demanded, "and if you won't tell me, we're not continuing this conversation."

"...he's my ex." Melanie fidgeted with her bracelet. "We dated in high school my senior year, his junior. Somehow, even as a junior, he convinced the entire senior class to hate me."

"That would have been three years ago," Evelyn pointed out, "and your story doesn't add up. Why would you keep going to book club after he joined?"

Melanie shrugged. "Because I'm a grade older. I got here first. Quitting felt like letting him win, and I'm too stubborn for that. He's the reason no one in book club likes me."

"No, you're the reason no one in book club likes you. You're just jealous of him and Erica." Evelyn stood up and walked back to the whiteboard.

"I'm serious, Evelyn. I'm trying to help you protect her. She won't listen to me, but she'll listen to you."

"And I'm not going to feed her your lies," Evelyn insisted. She continued her math on the whiteboard, sending a clear message that the conversation was over.

Melanie watched Evelyn write for a few seconds before she sighed and walked away.

Evelyn entered her statistics class and sat down. Her usual seat was taken. The room was twice as packed as normal; no one dared to skip class on test day. She methodically laid out two mechanical pencils, her favorite eraser, scratch paper, her water bottle, and her student ID. Her patience was tested as she waited for the exam to begin.

As soon as the professor set a test in front of her, her brain cells collectively lost all knowledge of statistics. Over the course of two hours, she tried to answer the questions, but every one was scattered with roadblocks, a step here and there that she couldn't remember how to solve. Her goal shifted from acing the test to simply finishing.

She gave her paper to the professor with only a few minutes left. Three-quarters of the students were still working.

At least she wasn't alone in her struggles.

Evelyn handed her debit card to the cashier at the drive through. Her thoughts oscillated between statistics and topology, her test and her homework, the past and the present. Although her brain was unwantedly active, her body was exhausted. She forced her eyelids open and her hand towards the window to take the bag of food being handed to her.

If tacos couldn't re-energize her, then all hope was lost.

She checked her buzzing phone at a red light on the way home.

David:
Are we still up for game night part 2?

Caroline:
I'm in

Aaron:
Me too!

Liam:
i'll bring the game

Aaron:
I'll bring snacks

Evelyn:
I'm grabbing dinner and finishing up my topology homework. Be there in two hours.

David:
Sounds good to me. See you soon!

A few tacos and topology problems later, Evelyn drove over to David's house. The street was filled with parked cars. She recognized several and inferred that she was the last to arrive. She walked inside and dumped her shoes, backpack, and jacket in the corner of the entryway.

"Evelyn! What's your favorite color?" Liam yelled at her from another room.

"Green. Why?"

"She can't be green; I'm green," Aaron said.

"Pick another color!" Liam yelled.

"Red," Evelyn said as she walked into the living room.

The coffee table was gone, and the couch and recliners were all pushed against the walls. In the center of the floor was a large map, surrounded by six colored baskets. Liam was sorting pieces into each. "This one is yours," he said as he placed a stack of cards into the red basket, "and the gray one is mine. Aaron claimed the green one. I'll give the orange one to Oliver, yellow to Caroline, and blue to David." He handed her six small drawstring bags and a larger bag of metal tokens that clinked together as she took it. "Can you put twenty-five in each bag, and one bag in each basket?"

"This game has a lot of pieces," Evelyn noted, looking at her red collection of coins and cards and figures.

Liam smiled. "It does! It's going to be great."

"Evelyn, you made it," Oliver said as he entered the room. He paused when he noticed the large map and countless trinkets scattered on the floor. "This looks painfully complicated." Nonetheless, he sat on the floor and helped Liam sort the cards. "How are your law school applications going?"

"They're... going," she responded.

"I'm guessing you haven't started," Oliver said.

"Well, I had a statistics test today, so I had to study a lot, and I had multiple homeworks on top of that. I'll work on it Friday."

"I'll hold you to that," Oliver warned.

They finished organizing the multitude of pieces needed for the game, and once everyone had taken their seat on the floor, Liam began explaining the rules. "The map here is the Kingdom of Marina—"

"Marinara? Are we making pizza?" Aaron asked.

Liam buried his face in his hands and stifled a laugh. "It's the Kingdom of Marina. We all live in this kingdom, in different regions as indicated by the colored pawns. The kingdom is ruled by a unanimously hated monarchy. Each of you is the leader of a group of rebels, named based on the color of the pieces in your basket. The names and special skills of your group are written on the card inside the envelope."

Evelyn peeked at her card. *You are the leader of the Scarlet Rebellion, known for their ruthless tactics and skilled assassins. You win if you kill the king and queen, and you're willing to kill anyone who stands in your way.*

"Your goal is to overthrow the monarchy," Liam continued. "Whoever can do so first wins."

"If we all have the same goal, why aren't we working together?" David asked.

Liam shrugged. "You're welcome to work together, but remember, whoever overthrows the monarchy will be seen by the people of Marina as saviors, and gain immense power and riches. Do you want to share your victory? Do you trust the other players not to stab you in the back?"

Oliver smiled. "Maybe your crazy strategy game will be more fun than I thought."

The Scarlet Rebellion was subtle and discrete; Evelyn made sure of it. Aaron and Oliver teamed up together, while David and Caroline fought each other. Liam's strategy was unknown, his moves seemingly random. Evelyn didn't take any action on the board. Instead, she quietly amassed a collection of cards, in-game resources she needed to transport her militia to the capital. She sat and counted the cards, calculating how many more rounds until she gathered all she needed.

David nudged Liam. "It's your turn."

"I attack the Scarlet Rebellion and steal their resources," Liam said, laying down the appropriate action and corresponding weapon cards.

Evelyn stared at the resources in front of her, trying desperately to find a way to salvage part of her ruined plan. She glared at Liam, and he smiled back. "Your strategy was good. Pacifism prevents you from making enemies, but collecting so many resources at once makes you a valuable target."

"You're good at this," Evelyn said, passing over the majority of her resource cards.

"How about we team up together?" Liam asked her.

"What's in it for you?" she inquired.

"It doubles the size of my militia, and you have nothing to lose. Most importantly, it's fun."

She shrugged. "Sure. Let's go for it."

From there, the strategy was fairly straightforward. David and Caroline were already weakened from battling each other, meaning the other four beat them to the capital. Ultimately, Evelyn and Liam were able to defeat the king and queen before Aaron and Oliver.

They had almost won the game. Evelyn, however, still had one more trick lying in wait. She looked at the assassin card in her hand, giving her the power to kill Liam and take the victory alone.

"You know you could win with that, right?" Liam said.

She nodded. "I read the card. I know how it works." She tossed it back in the red basket. "I don't have to play it. The rules say we can both win."

"I've been waiting all game for a chance to play my assassin card against Aaron! You get the chance and you don't even take it?" Oliver said in shock.

Aaron gasped in an over-dramatized manner. "You were going to betray me?"

"That's part of the game," Caroline said. "My own boyfriend turned against me."

"I only betrayed you because I knew you'd betray me later," David said in defense.

Caroline smiled. "You know me so well."

"Well, Evelyn and I win," Liam said. He looked at Evelyn. He smiled at her, not just with his lips, but with his eyes. "Let's clean up the game."

Evelyn walked through the winding halls of her dorm and found her room. She sat down on her bed and looked at the pictures of her family hanging on the wall. The day her mom helped her move in, Avery insisted on tagging along. Like a typical little sister, she spent seconds helping unpack and hours exploring the building and making executive decisions about where Evelyn's decor should go. Avery was the one who pinned all the photos to the wall. She talked all day about how Evelyn was such a genius, as if getting accepted into college was on par with winning a Nobel Prize. She told Evelyn that she would be "the best lawyer in the history of ever."

Evelyn wished her sister had been right.

She hadn't thought about the LSAT all day. The sudden realization brought both joy and concern. It was nice not to worry about law school, but eventually, she needed to worry. It was an inevitable problem she would eventually be forced to face. Nonetheless, the board game was a nice break. For just a few hours, she didn't have to figure out life after graduation. She simply had to defeat a monarchy, a seemingly easy task by comparison. Being the leader of the Scarlet Rebellion, a growing uprising with cunning and callousness, was a lot more fun than being Evelyn, a senior in college with no clue how to handle life's pitfalls.

She opened the group chat.

Evelyn:

I had fun tonight. We should play again.

Liam:

did you know there's a sequel game? i'll buy it!

She turned off the lights, drowning the room in moonlit shadows that stole her view of the photos. If she couldn't see Avery's joy in the pictures, she didn't have to imagine Avery's disappointment when she failed to become the lawyer she promised to be.

Friday, September 20

Another Friday meant another day at the boba tea shop. Piper waved as Evelyn walked in. "Good morning! Do you want the usual?"

Evelyn nodded and swiped her card to pay. "Thanks." She sat down in her normal seat. Slowly but surely, she marked items off her to-do list. After several hours of reading monotonous textbook chapters and solving obscure math problems, she finally reached the last item on the list: apply for law school.

She wasn't ready for that yet. She had plenty of caffeine to keep her going, but she didn't have the emotional capacity to handle it.

Instead, she resorted to productive procrastination: her favorite method of guilt-free stalling. She took out Melanie's manuscript and a red pen and started reading. Despite her frustration with the author, she couldn't deny her interest in the book. The setting was intriguing: a futuristic monarchy in a world with both technology and magic. The plot was full of dramatic politics, uncertain allies, and copious mystery. Nonetheless, Evelyn's favorite part of the book was the characters. Every one was built with a multifaceted personality, a wide range of emotions and complex motivations. The protagonist, Adelaide, was a bit of a rebel, yet also a realist. Evelyn loved her integrity, her loyalty, and her determination. Her best friend, Livia, was quirky and energetic, and the dynamic of their friendship was fun to read.

When Evelyn finally looked up from the manuscript, over two hours had passed. She promised herself she'd start law school applications at home after running a few errands. She packed up her belongings, waved goodbye to Piper, and got in her car. Pop music blared on the radio while she toured the town: picking up alfredo sauce at the grocery store, trying a new coffee shop nearby, and printing more photos for the wall of her room. She finally headed back to campus in the evening, where she popped in her earbuds, cooked pasta for dinner, washed a load of dirty towels, and went for a walk around sunset. Finally, after a long day of music and mindless tasks, she looked at her to-do list. There was only one item left.

She erased it from the list and went to sleep.

Seeing Through Shattered Glass
by Melanie Oaken

Chapter 1

Technology is working within the constraints of reality to create things that seem impossible. Magic is bending reality to your will to create things that are impossible.

Adelaide, like most of the population, had a healthy fear of magic. Altering reality did not come without a cost. So instead, Adelaide studied technology; specifically, computer science. Her phone always contained at least 3 homemade apps for alpha testing. Livia always gave her a hard time about starting apps and never finishing them.

But it wasn't her fault. Her free time was occupied with her other hobby: live streaming. At the age of 19, she had built a decent audience. To her surprise, they never seemed to get tired of her commentary on current events.

Adelaide looked around the room

Notes:

Magic vs tech sounds interesting...

I think this should be a colon, not a semi-colon?

at her makeshift studio. It was hard to believe that they had come so far from the small online news account they had started when they were only teenagers. Adelaide's mom would argue that they were still teenagers now, but Livia said 19 doesn't count.

"Three, two, one… action." Livia counted down as the cameras started. Adelaide smiled. "Thanks for tuning into the unplanned episode today. As you could probably guess, I want to talk about the announcement that the king and queen made this morning. Yes, I know it seems kind and gracious and whatever. But in reality, they're just trying to save what little sympathy and adoration they have left. If you haven't heard, the monarchy announced that they're going to build a council to represent the people of Kaliana. In truth, it's not representative of us if they get to pick who's on the council! Of course they're simply going to pick people who agree with their procedures and

Notes:

This is a lot of information in the first four paragraphs. It might be too quick. Not sure.

You stated her age twice in two paragraphs back to back. I would pick one or the other.

Oh drama, you love drama…

4

Sunday, September 22

E velyn added her shoes and backpack to the cluttered mess on the floor of David's house. Even from the entryway, she could hear the familiar sound of debate coming from the other room. She sought the source and found the guys huddled in the living room. Caroline, wisely, was nowhere to be found.

"Alright, idiots, what's going on here?" Evelyn asked. The guys quieted down and all turned to look at her in unison.

"Would the world be more aesthetically pleasing if cars could fly?" Oliver asked. They stared in anticipation of her verdict.

She stared back quizzically. "What?"

"If cars could fly, then we wouldn't need roads partitioning every block. We could have more grass and more trees, and we could get rid of the crazy highway intersections with bridges that look like a bowl of spaghetti from overhead," Aaron argued.

David laughed. "I'm surprised you even know what the word 'partitioning' means."

"But then there would be cars blocking the sun and the clouds! The sky would be forever ruined! At least planes are sparse and hard to see. I don't want to fill every sunset with a confetti of cars," Liam rebutted.

"As you can see, this is a very important topic," Oliver told Evelyn. "What do you think?"

"I think I need to find Caroline." She left, ignoring the pleas for her answer to the absurd question.

Caroline stood in the kitchen, stirring a cup of hot chocolate. "Did you let the boys drag you into their debate?"

"Of course not. How long have they been discussing this?"

Caroline shrugged. "About half an hour."

"I'm not even surprised."

Oliver joined the girls, grabbing a can of soda out of the fridge. "How are the law school applications going?"

"I still haven't started if that's what you're asking," Evelyn said.

If Oliver had any emotional response, any care about her applications, he didn't show it on his face. "Do you still study at that boba tea shop on Fridays?"

"Every week."

"Good. I'll meet you there." He closed the fridge door and left, presumably to rejoin the discussion about flying cars.

"What in the world was that about?" Caroline asked.

"I have no earthly idea," Evelyn said. "I guess we should join them. Maybe we can convince them to pause their debate and start the game."

Clarissa and Jareth approached the Lister mansion again. This time, they didn't sneak through the alleys and spy on the guards to configure a plan. This time, they were prepared, and they made their presence known.

The guards watched like vipers coiled seconds before a strike. One left his post to approach Clarissa and Jareth. "Halt. Who are you? What business do you have here?"

Clarissa smiled, wrapping her arm around Jareth's. "My name is Clarissa Amica, and this is my boyfriend. I'm here to see Kinsley. Can we talk to her?"

"I've never seen you around," the guard said. He turned to another guard nearby. "Have you ever seen these two?" he asked. The second guard shook his head.

"We met Kinsley on one of her little escapades outside the mansion. We're not really at liberty to discuss the details," Clarissa explained with a wink.

The guard chuckled. "Dumb kid never stays out of trouble."

Clarissa felt Jareth's muscles relax as the guard's stern exterior broke.

"I'll go tell her you're here. What did you say your name was again?"

"Clarissa. Tell her we have a gift for her."

The guards nodded at each other in unspoken agreement. One wandered inside the mansion to find Kinsley while the other carefully watched Jareth and Clarissa.

"The garden here is beautiful." Clarissa let go of Jareth's arm and wandered the path. "Look at the flowers."

"Absolutely beautiful," Jareth said. His eyes focused not on the plants but on Clarissa.

A few moments later, the guard returned. "You may enter. Stay with me; I'll take you to Kinsley. Don't try anything stupid. Kinsley is the only one allowed to cause trouble around here."

Two guards escorted them into the mansion, down a long corridor and to an office. It was smaller than the large foyer they entered through or the library and the dining room they passed in the hall. Still, the room was bigger than any Clarissa had seen outside of Caridelle. The office was lined with beautiful wooden shelves filled with aesthetic trinkets and books stacked in sporadic decorative groups. The back wall held a large fireplace with a Lister family portrait hanging above, displaying Kinsley as a toddler being held between her parents. In front of the fireplace was a large wooden desk full of elegant hand-carved swirls and other small lavish and useless details. On top of the desk sat Kinsley; her brown eyes lit up as Clarissa entered. "Clarissa, bestie, it's so good to see you! Guards, you can go. Close the door on your way out."

The guards nodded and followed her instructions without question.

As soon as the large door slammed closed, Kinsley's smile disappeared, and she glared at the couple in front of her. "Alright, Clarissa, if that's even your real name. What do you want?"

"I brought you a gift." Clarissa handed the small ornate box to Kinsley, who opened it to see the scrolls. Kinsley's eyes lit up again.

"Thank you for bringing this to me. I'm excited to add it to my collection."

"Don't you mean return it to your collection?" Clarissa asked.

Kinsley's head tilted slightly. "Return? What do you mean?"

"We were told this box was stolen from you. We came to return it."

Kinsley giggled. "Is that what Jemma told you? She's such a creative little storyteller."

"Tell us the truth," Jareth demanded.

"The truth is, I needed someone to steal this for me." She tossed Jareth a small bag giving the familiar sound of coins clinking together. "Thank you, my friends."

"We're not thieves. We didn't agree to steal for you." Jareth tried to take the box out of Kinsley's hand, but she dodged him.

"What's your name?" she asked.

"Jareth," he answered, his voice filled with hesitation.

"Jareth, I like you. You seem nice. And I think it's cute that you have integrity. I've never really understood that sort of thing myself." She locked the box away in a drawer in the desk and sat in the chair, twirling her strawberry blonde hair between her fingers. "But, Jareth, it's not my fault that you took on a quest that didn't meet your moral standards. You brought me the box, I paid you, and now it belongs to me."

"We were lied to." Jareth took a step towards Kinsley, but Clarissa grabbed his arm.

"I'm not an 'honesty' type of girl. But Jareth, I'm not the one who lied to you." Kinsley leaned forward, propping her elbows on the desk. "You have two options: you can either leave here as an ally or be escorted out as an adversary."

Jareth glared at her. "I hate you."

Clarissa pushed herself in front of Jareth, looking him in the eyes. "Leave."

Jareth took a deep breath, glared at Clarissa, and walked towards the door. "I'll wait right outside the room." He paused for a second to glare back at Kinsley. "Don't you dare hurt her." He stepped out of the room, the large wooden door slamming shut behind him.

Kinsley laughed. "Your boyfriend is a little protective."

"He's not my boyfriend. That was just a ruse for the guards." Clarissa pulled a chair from the side of the room and sat to face Kinsley. "Listen, I'm sorry about Jareth. I came here to make friends, not enemies."

"We can be friends, as long as you keep your partner from crossing me. But I'm sure that'll be easy for you. You seem like the type of girl who often gets her way."

"It takes one to know one," Clarissa replied.

Kinsley chuckled. "Who are you anyways? What guild are you with?"

Clarissa shrugged. "No guild. I'm just a kid from Mistcoast."

"Mistcoast?"

"It's a port city to the east."

Kinsley leaned back in her chair. "And how long have you been stealing stuff for strangers?"

Clarissa shrugged again. "This is the first."

"So how does a kid like you end up crossing Arydia for a quest like this?"

"That's a story for another day." Clarissa stood from her chair and headed towards the door. "Let us know if you need anything. We'll be in town for another day or so. Do you know how to cast a message spell?"

"I'm not really into magic. It takes too much practice. Too much studying. But if I need something, I know how to find you."

Clarissa nodded to her and let the door close between them. Jareth leaned against the wall, arms crossed, glaring at the door as if the wood could be hurt by his spite.

"Let's get out of here," Clarissa said. She spoke gently, her words as soft as her touch on Jareth's arm.

Jareth's body and gaze didn't budge. "Jemma lied to us."

Clarissa nodded. "I know. But we need to find somewhere else to be mad. We can't stay here."

Jareth sighed. "You're right. Let's go."

"Caroline!" Liam yelled her name from across the table.

"Wait, I thought we were stealing from thieves! Did we steal from decent people? Are we wanted criminals now?" Oliver exclaimed, looking to David for an answer.

David shrugged. "You'll have to wait and find out."

"We have to wait until next week?" Aaron yelled.

Caroline simply smiled, her grin unwavering in the chaos.

"You lied to us," Evelyn accused, but she mirrored Caroline's grin on her own face.

"I didn't lie to you. Jemma did," Caroline said.

Liam laughed. "You don't get to blame your characters for your actions."

"Okay, so maybe I lied. But what did you expect? I'm a Gemini."

"You don't get to blame your star sign either," Oliver said, rolling his eyes.

"Of course I do. I'm a Gemini." Caroline went to the kitchen to pack up the leftovers from dinner.

Aaron grinned and looked around at the group. Evelyn watched him hesitantly. She recognized that smile; Aaron had many facial expressions, but this one in particular

THE LEGEND OF EVELYN

always came before a scheme. He motioned for the group to huddle close.

"We should ambush Caroline when she tries to leave. I have my arsenal of Nerf guns in my car."

Liam, David, and Oliver nodded in excitement.

"Why in the world do you have an arsenal of Nerf guns?" Evelyn asked.

"Why don't you?" Aaron replied, leaving Evelyn speechless.

They snuck out the back door, gathered their weapons, and hid behind bushes and trees in the yard. Eventually, Caroline walked outside, searching for her missing friends. On Aaron's cue, they all attacked, running and shooting and laughing.

The stars watched silently as the Gemini was pelted with Nerf bullets.

Monday, September 23

Evelyn dragged her feet along the sidewalk to class. Her constant sipping of coffee was interrupted only by the occasional yawn. As much as she loved game nights, they were constantly depriving her of valuable time. She couldn't afford to lose sleep to participate in fictional senseless escapades, yet the chaos of their game was a needed escape from reality. Clarissa's adventures, although fictional, brought a sense of delight that Evelyn's boring life never could. She couldn't afford to lose her brightest spark of joy.

She walked into the classroom filled with half-asleep students. "Laplace's Equation" was written across the top of the whiteboard. Today was going to be a long day.

"Evelyn!" Erica found Evelyn on the way to the library. "How are you?"

"I'm good. How are you? How was the second date?"

Erica's eyes sparkled, and her smile stretched from ear to ear. "It was so nice. Beckett is amazing. I have the best boyfriend ever."

"So he's reached boyfriend status now?"

Erica shrugged. "Well, we didn't really talk about it, but he introduced me to his friends as his girlfriend."

"You met his friends?" Every answer Erica gave left Evelyn with even more questions.

"Yeah, we went bowling last night for our second date. His friends wanted to join, so they came with us."

In Evelyn's opinion, it didn't count as a date if his friends joined, but there was no need to correct her. "Did you have fun?"

"Of course! Beckett's friend Aiden won the first game, and Beckett won the next two. I didn't win any of them. I don't think bowling is my forte."

"The important part is that you enjoyed it."

"I did! It was so much fun. Beckett!" Erica ran into the library as soon as she saw him. He wrapped his arms around her in a hug, whispering something in her ear to make her laugh.

Evelyn sighed. The concept of dating was strange. In theory, dating was a train ride that started at infatuation and ended in marriage, except most trains crashed before reaching their destination. Nonetheless, society loved to buy more train tickets, go on more dates, and repeatedly watch their hearts shatter like glass.

Evelyn found a seat as book club started. The distracted lovebirds paid her little attention. Most of the group was talkative except for Melanie, who was staring at Erica, who was staring at Beckett. Evelyn studied Melanie's face, trying carefully to read her expression. She expected jealousy, but that didn't seem right. Was it anger? No, it was sadness, with a touch of pity. Eventually, Melanie noticed Evelyn watching her. Melanie looked away with embarrassment, training her eyes on the floor instead.

As soon as book club was over, Evelyn approached Erica, stealing her attention from the boy. "Do you want to go to lunch today?"

"I can't. I told Beckett I'd help him with the chemistry homework."

"Have fun. Stay out of trouble." Evelyn gave her a smile and walked off, the smile fading the moment her back was to Erica.

Evelyn kicked off her shoes and crashed on the couch after her last class of the day. She laid her head on the armrest, inspecting every bump on the popcorn ceiling. Bethany wandered out of her room. "Can you take me to the grocery store?"

"I'm busy throwing a pity party."

"Please, Evelyn?" Bethany begged. "Please?" Her tone showed her desperation. Maybe she had run out of something vital, like toilet paper or deodorant, or maybe she needed something last minute for a class project. Evelyn didn't care to ask. She grabbed her keys and headed towards the door, Bethany following behind.

They drove silently to the store, with Evelyn stewing in annoyance and Bethany wringing her hands in her lap. They parked without a word and walked into the store. Evelyn tried to engage in small talk with a comment about the forecasted rain, but her roommate didn't respond. Bethany picked up a box of blueberry muffin mix, a container of vegetable oil, and a carton of eggs, then paid for the items and walked back to the car.

Evelyn sat down in the driver's seat, hiding her frustration at the unnecessary muffins that had dragged her to the store. "Blueberry muffins," she said, the phrase leaving her mouth less like a statement and more like a question. Bethany still insisted on silence. Evelyn stopped at a red light, took a deep breath to suppress her anger, and turned to look at her roommate in the passenger seat. In the dim light of the street lamps, she could see silent tears falling down Bethany's cheeks.

Evelyn didn't push for an answer, but Bethany eventually provided one as Evelyn put the car in park. "My mom used to make me blueberry muffins before every big test at school," Bethany said quietly. "When she passed away, I started baking the muffins for myself." The girls sat frozen in silence. The tears streaking down Bethany's face were the only proof of passing time. Eventually, Evelyn placed a gentle hand on Bethany's shoulder, and suddenly, Bethany tackled her in a hug. Evelyn embraced her, rubbing her roommate's back while she cried into her shoulder. "My mom loved my brothers so much, even when they moved out of the house and made stupid life choices. But I was the baby of the family. I was always her little girl. She called me her little ray of sunshine." Bethany continued to sob as she told Evelyn stories of her mom. From the spaghetti dinners they cooked to the adventures traveling the country, there were so many moments, so many memories. Evelyn sat quietly and listened until Bethany noticed the time and became silent. She had been talking for almost an hour. "I'm so sorry."

"Don't be," Evelyn said. "I'm always glad to talk to you." Evelyn stepped out of the car. "Let's go bake some muffins."

"I thought you had a pity party to throw," Bethany said.

Evelyn shrugged. "There'll always be more time for pity parties later."

Tuesday, September 24

Liam:

who wants to play video games tonight? meet at my apartment at 6.

Oliver:

sounds good to me

David:

I can't, I'm busy

Aaron:

I'll be there!

Caroline:

I'll come too!!! Watch out, Oliver, I've been practicing :)

Evelyn stared at her phone screen. She wanted to be there, to forget about school, to get decimated in a fighting game that meant nothing at the end of the day. Unfortunately, the length of her to-do list said she didn't have time.

Evelyn:

I have to study :(Maybe next time

She claimed her table in the honors lounge and unpacked her notes. Melanie sat in the corner, glancing up at her occasionally. Evelyn didn't acknowledge her; she didn't have the capacity for drama today.

She opened her essay on her laptop and started writing. The assignment was to write a research paper about use cases for artificial intelligence. Unsurprisingly, she chose to write about AI applications for lawyers.

The steps for research were simple: find an article, read it, and take some notes. Find another article, read it, and decide it's useless. Find another article, get blocked by a paywall, and pirate it instead. The work was slow but easy. Writing, on the other hand, was slow and painful. As soon as she opened a blank document, she couldn't remember a single word in the English language. She stared at the empty page before finally remembering it needed to be in APA format. That was a good starting point. She wrote her name, class, professor, date, and a line that read "Insert Title Here". Then she moved on to page two, and suddenly, she was stuck again with a blank mind staring at a blank page.

The honors room around her was eerily quiet with the exception of Melanie typing away on her keyboard. Her manuscript proved she was a better writer than Evelyn would ever be. It wasn't fair.

"Is something wrong?" Melanie asked, breaking Evelyn's trance of thought and her blank stare in Melanie's direction.

"No, sorry. Just trying to write an essay. I can't figure out where to start."

"Try starting with an oddly specific detail," Melanie suggested.

"How does that help?" Evelyn asked.

"It's just another angle to try. Typically, we write an overall statement and then use details to back it up. But sometimes, I like to start with the details and build the scene out from there. Maybe I start by describing a character's dress and the way it moves when she walks. Then I describe the hallway she's walking through. Then I explain where she's headed and why. Begin with the details and build out. It doesn't always work, but it's worth a try."

"Thanks." Evelyn looked back at her laptop and started to write. One detail turned into a single sentence, which slowly turned into a single point, which developed into a single page. She was making progress—slow, messy progress that desperately needed massive revisions, but progress nonetheless.

She adopted the honors lounge as her home for most of the day, only leaving for class and the occasional snack break. She was determined to, one-by-one, check items off her to-do list. After working on her essay for a few hours, she moved on to her topology homework, and after seven painful hours, she finally finished. She took a pen and added a satisfying little check mark in the box. One task done.

Twelve more to go.

Her efforts seemed futile. It was already 6 p.m., and she had barely made a dent in her list.

Maybe she just needed a change of scenery. She packed up her bags and headed towards the library. As she walked across campus, her phone vibrated. The group chat had sent a picture of their favorite video game, where Oliver as Thunder Bolt had single-handedly beat Aaron, Caroline, and Liam combined.

Homework was too hard, too frustrating, too depressing. Video games seemed easier and meaningless.

Evelyn:

> Looks like you need some help. Mind if I join?

With Evelyn's help, Aaron, Caroline, and Liam finally beat Oliver. Caroline wasn't lying when she said she'd been practicing; she had improved greatly. Oliver, however, had been practicing too, and he, unlike Caroline, had nothing better to do with his time than commit endless hours to a worthless skill.

"Good job. You finally beat me," Oliver said. The others didn't gloat about their victory like they normally would. Winning four to one didn't seem like an achievement to be proud of.

"We'll beat you again in a minute," Liam said as he stepped onto his balcony to answer his ringing phone.

"How many hours have you spent on this unproductive game?" Evelyn asked. She grabbed a soda out of the fridge and joined Oliver on the couch.

"It doesn't track my time, but I'd guess a few thousand," Oliver said. "Speaking of unproductive, how are your law school applications going?"

"Are you going to ask that every single time we meet?" Evelyn said.

Oliver shrugged. "Only until you start on them."

Evelyn sighed in frustration. "I'm a full-time student. I have five demanding classes, a Saturday job, an adopted freshman and roommate to take care of, and you idiots to put up with. I don't have time to apply to law schools that won't accept me anyways."

Oliver rolled his eyes. "Then apply to some that will. If it makes you feel better, start with some schools that you're almost guaranteed to get accepted to. 166 isn't a bad score."

"How would you even know?" She slammed her drink on the coffee table. "You never had to worry about anything like this. You just graduated and got a job. It was easy for—"

"It wasn't easy for me. I had a 2.6 GPA, no job experience, and no family to support me. I started working in fast food the day after I graduated just to afford groceries. I lived on Liam's couch for months. I got rejected from almost 30 jobs before I found one, and then they wanted me to move to California where I'd have no friends and couldn't afford rent. So I applied for another 80 or so jobs, got rejected again and again, until finally I found my job as a middle school PE teacher that pays me just enough to split rent with my horribly obnoxious roommate. It wasn't easy for me, and it's still not easy, but I survived. You, princess, have a world of opportunities in front of you, and you won't take your eyes off the closed door long enough to notice all the open ones."

Evelyn stared at Oliver, speechless. Aaron slowly offered Oliver a controller. The menu music of their favorite racing game interrupted the silent tension.

Oliver sighed. "Sure," he said, answering the unspoken question and taking the controller.

"Finally, something I can win at." Aaron picked up his own controller and selected his favorite bright red sports car.

The cars zoomed down the track, racing almost as fast as Evelyn's typical thoughts, though in this moment, her thoughts were frozen, buffering, unable to compute.

She gave up on thinking and immersed herself in the game, the fake cars racing down the fake track, the fake crowd cheering, the fake scores rising. Reverie was simpler than reality.

Thursday, September 26

Erica:

Lunch today?

I miss you! I haven't seen you in a whole 3 days! :(

Have you ever tried sushi?

It sounds weird

But I kind of want to try it

But I have no clue what to order

Evelyn:

I have a test at noon, how about dinner?

Erica:

Ok, let me check with Beckett, I think he might have had plans for us

Nevermind, he just has plans with his friends, dinner it is!

Evelyn drove to the freshman dorm across campus. "So you've never had sushi?" Evelyn asked as Erica sat in the passenger seat.

Erica shook her head. "Nope. My parents don't like it, so we never ate it."

Evelyn laughed. "Well, today's the day. If you hate it, we'll get some chicken nuggets on the way home."

They drove to the restaurant and sat down at a table in the corner. Evelyn ordered a small variety of sushi rolls for Erica to try.

"I had another date with Beckett last night," Erica said, smiling at the memory. "We had a picnic at the park near his house."

"How was it?" Evelyn asked.

"It was beautiful. I brought sandwiches and strawberries and lemonade and we just sat and talked for hours." She went on and on describing the details of the date, the topics of conversation, and the surroundings of the park. She gave Evelyn an entire play-by-play of the evening. By the time she finished, the waitress had already returned with their food.

Erica fumbled with chopsticks until Evelyn handed her a fork. "Try a bite of this first," Evelyn said, pointing. "It's a California roll."

Erica took a bite. "It's... weird. I think I like it, but it's weird."

"That makes sense. Try the cucumber roll next."

Erica took another bite, and her eyes widened.

"What's that face mean? Do you like it? Hate it?" Evelyn asked.

Erica shook her head. "I just realized I forgot to tell you about the end of the date!"

"The end?" Evelyn asked.

Erica nodded. "So... we kissed."

Evelyn was surprised, completely caught off guard, but she didn't let her face show it. "How did it happen?"

"Well, we were talking about dating. He asked if I'd had a boyfriend before, and I said no. Somehow the topic of kissing came up, and I told him I'd never kissed anyone, and then in the middle of my sentence he just kissed me. It just happened. It was adorable."

Evelyn took a deep breath. "Erica, did you want to kiss him?"

"I don't know. He's my boyfriend. Isn't that just a thing you're supposed to do when you're dating?"

Evelyn held back a flood of emotions, comments, and chastisements. "No, Erica. Dating doesn't mean you have to kiss him. I have so many questions. First off: just kissing?"

Erica nodded. "Just kissing... for now."

Evelyn couldn't help but sigh aloud at that statement. "You don't have to kiss him if you don't want to."

"Of course I want to!" Erica sounded like she was trying to convince herself just as much as Evelyn. "I like him! He's my boyfriend! Besides—"

"You've been dating for two weeks, Erica."

"—his friends would have given him such a hard time if he had a girlfriend who wouldn't even kiss him, and—"

"I don't care about his stupid friends!"

"—I really like him, and that's all that matters, so—"

"There's so much more that matters!"

"—stop trying to protect me!" Erica glared at her. "You're just jealous. You haven't been on a date in years, and you're just jealous."

You're just jealous. The words echoed in Evelyn's mind, not in Erica's voice, but in her own. Her mind flashed back to her conversation with Melanie in the honors lounge, talking about Erica and Beckett. *You're just jealous.*

"I don't think Beckett's a good guy, Erica."

"Shut up." Erica stared down at her crossed arms.

"Melanie tried to warn you, and I told her to stay away. But I think she was right."

"Beckett says Melanie is an insecure liar. He told me not to listen to her."

"How do you know he's not a liar?" Evelyn asked.

"Because he's my boyfriend! I trust him!" Erica stuffed another piece of sushi in her mouth. "Take me home. I don't want to talk to you."

"Erica, please. Calm—"

"Shut up." She stood up and walked out of the restaurant.

Evelyn found the waitress, paid for the check, and packed up the food in a to-go box. When she walked outside, Erica was nowhere to be found. Evelyn's phone vibrated.

Erica

I'm taking the bus home. Leave me alone.

She looked across the parking lot and noticed Erica walking down the sidewalk towards the nearest bus stop. In theory, she could catch up, but it wouldn't be beneficial. If Erica wanted to be left alone, stopping her would just add fuel to the burning bridge.

Friday, September 27

Oliver:

i'll meet you at the boba shop at 5

"Strawberry green tea with crystal boba?" Piper asked as Evelyn entered the boba shop. Evelyn nodded, and Piper handed her the drink she had already prepared before Evelyn walked in the door.

Evelyn sat down at her table, unpacking her laptop. She had 3 hours of silence to finish as much as she could before Oliver interrupted her. Thankfully, her morning had been productive, so she had just two assignments left to conquer.

With a pencil in one hand and boba tea in the other, she started to work. The shop was quiet and slow. Calm piano melodies played in the background. Customers entered and exited at their leisure. An occasional breeze brushed past each time the door opened. The atmosphere made even statistics problems feel serene. That was, of course, until Oliver walked in.

"Good afternoon! What would you like?" Piper asked.

He stared at the menu, trying to decipher the list of teas and smoothies, bobas and jellies, snacks and desserts. Finally he turned to Evelyn. "What do you get?"

"Strawberry green tea with crystal boba," Piper answered before Evelyn got a chance.

Oliver chuckled. "Wow, you really do come here often, Evelyn. I'll take the same thing." He paid for his drink and sat down across from Evelyn. "Alright, which law school are we applying to first?"

"I'm trying to derive the variance of the sum of two normal distributions."

"I have no clue what that means."

She scribbled the last line of the proof and turned the paper around to show him.

"Is that English?" Oliver asked.

"That's an integral sign, and that's a lowercase sigma, which is a Greek letter, and that's pi, which is also a Greek letter." She pointed to various symbols on the paper.

"Math language. Got it. Law school applications are in English, right? Which one are we starting with?"

Evelyn sighed. "Seriously, Oliver, I'm not ready for this."

"Procrastination is just delaying pain. You've been avoiding this for weeks, princess."

"I don't even know where to start."

TESSA MARIE

"Let's start with an easy one. Are there any schools that you're almost guaranteed to get admitted to?"

"Sure, the bad ones," she said. "What's the point in applying to those?"

"Think of it as practice for applying to the good ones."

Oliver was annoying, but his logic was foolproof. "Fine. We'll start there."

The application began with the facts: her name, date of birth, social security number, address, and so on. She uploaded her transcript and wrote responses to the short-answer questions. Oliver helped her talk through each step and listened to her rant about the stupidly long process and poorly designed user interface. For the most part, he was quiet while Evelyn worked diligently. She hated to admit it, but he was right. All she needed to complete the applications was a little encouragement and a friend to keep her accountable.

The last step was her personal statement. She had started on it weeks ago but hadn't yet perfected it. "I can't submit the application yet, Oliver. This part takes a long time and a lot of revisions."

"You made progress. That's the important part, princess."

She rolled her eyes. "You're never going to let that nickname go, are you?"

"Do you remember the day you got that nickname?" Oliver asked.

"Of course I do. I've never been in so much pain." She laughed, and Oliver did too.

122

"It was a great day. Me and Liam and Aaron and you. Nothing bonds friends like a trip to the hospital."

"I hated that ER. It was so loud and cramped and everyone was sick. I felt like I was going to catch five diseases by the time I walked out of there."

"That's what you get for hurting your ankle," Oliver said.

Despite the pain involved, the memory made her smile. They were helping Liam move into his new apartment; he had promised them pizza in exchange for physical labor, a trade that freshman Aaron and Evelyn gladly accepted. They carried box after box up to the third floor. Evelyn was a little overconfident and took a box heavier than she could handle. The large box blocked her view of the steps. Her lack of visibility and lack of muscle created a recipe for disaster; she tripped, tumbling down the stairs along with the box. When she landed, her ankle throbbed, and it couldn't bear any weight. She knew immediately that the injury was severe. She was later grateful it turned out to be only a bad sprain.

"I was crying so much. You picked me up and carried me to Liam's car. I think Aaron was going to, but I was too heavy."

"No, Aaron was just too weak," Oliver corrected. "Charisma is his strong suit, not strength."

"I'm glad he was there," Evelyn said. "It was comforting to have a friend. I mean, you and Liam were friends too, but I knew him better than you two at that point."

"I'm glad he was there too," Oliver said. "It took all three of us to take care of you in the ER. You were needy!" he teased. "We had to carry you into the hospital, then move you to a more comfortable chair, then call your mom, get you a snack, and another snack, and some chocolate, and a book, and a blanket—"

"I was spoiled, I know," Evelyn interrupted with a laugh. "That's why you nicknamed me princess."

"That's why I nicknamed you princess," Oliver confirmed.

Evelyn sighed. "That was a good day. I was miserable at the time, but looking back, it makes me laugh."

"Hindsight is 20/20." Oliver checked his phone. "I should head out. My middle school football players are all going to the high school game tonight. I promised the high school coach I'd keep them out of trouble." He headed towards the door.

"Have fun," Evelyn said. She put her laptop away. "By the way, today, meeting for boba…" She hesitated before asking her question. "This wasn't a date, right?"

Oliver laughed—a genuine laugh that shook his whole body. "No. Of course not. I wouldn't date my best friend's crush."

Piper chuckled as the door closed behind him.

6. $X \sim N(X, X)$ and $Y \sim N(Y, Y)$. Use convolutions to prove the mean and variance of $Z = X + Y$.

$$f_X(x) = \frac{1}{\sqrt{2\pi}\,\sigma_x} \qquad \text{and} \qquad f_y(y) = \frac{1}{\sqrt{2\pi}\,\sigma_y}$$

$$f_z(z) = \int_{-\infty}^{\infty} f_X(x)\, f_y(z-x)\, dx = \int_{-\infty}^{\infty} \frac{1}{\sqrt{2\pi}\,\sigma_x}\, e^{-\frac{(x-\mu_x)^2}{2\sigma_x^2}} \, \frac{1}{\sqrt{2\pi}\,\sigma_y}\, e^{-\frac{(z-x-\mu_y)^2}{2\sigma_y^2}}$$

$$= \int_{-\infty}^{\infty} \frac{1}{\sqrt{2\pi}\,\sigma_x \sqrt{2\pi}\,\sigma_y}\, e^{-\frac{x^2(\sigma_x^2+\sigma_y^2)-2x(\sigma_x^2(z-\mu_y)+\sigma_y^2\mu_x)+\sigma_x^2(z^2+\mu_y^2-2z\mu_y)+\sigma_y^2\mu_x^2}{2\sigma_x^2\sigma_y^2}} \, dx$$

$$\text{let } \sigma_z = \sqrt{\sigma_x + \sigma_y}$$

$$f_z(z) = \int_{-\infty}^{\infty} \frac{1}{\sqrt{2\pi}\,\sigma_z \sqrt{2\pi}\,\frac{\sigma_x\sigma_y}{\sigma_z}}\, e^{-\frac{x^2-2x\,\frac{\sigma_x^2(z-\mu_y)+\sigma_y^2\mu_x}{\sigma_z^2}+\frac{\sigma_x^2(z^2+\mu_y^2-2z\mu_y)+\sigma_y^2\mu_x^2}{\sigma_z^2}}{2\left(\frac{\sigma_x\sigma_y}{\sigma_z}\right)^2}} \, dx$$

$$= \frac{1}{\sqrt{2\pi}\,\sigma_z}\, e^{-\frac{(z-(\mu_x+\mu_y))^2}{2\sigma_z^2}} \int_{-\infty}^{\infty} \frac{1}{\sqrt{2\pi}\,\frac{\sigma_x\sigma_y}{\sigma_z}}\, e^{-\frac{\left(x^2-2x\,\frac{\sigma_x^2(z-\mu_y)+\sigma_y^2\mu_x}{\sigma_z^2}\right)^2}{2\left(\frac{\sigma_x\sigma_y}{\sigma_z}\right)^2}} \, dx$$

The integrand represents a normal distribution, so the integral equals to 1.

Therefore, $f_z(z) = \frac{1}{\sqrt{2\pi}\,\sigma_z}\, e^{-\frac{(z-(\mu_x+\mu_y))^2}{2\sigma_z^2}}$

So the mean is $\mu_x + \mu_y$ and the variance is $\sigma_x + \sigma_y$.

5

Sunday, September 29

E velyn blared the music in her car, but even at full volume, it couldn't drown out the sound bite stuck in her head.

I wouldn't date my best friend's crush.

The words repeated, a broken record in her mind, but she tried her best to tune it out. Tonight was game night, an opportunity for Evelyn to forget about herself and her friends and her friend's crushes and focus on Clarissa instead.

She walked into David's house, waving at the group. "Hey, Evelyn. How was your weekend?" Oliver asked.

"Pretty busy. I had a lot of overthinking to do."

"About what?" Oliver played ignorant, but she knew he wasn't dumb. She walked past him into the living room without answering.

"Evelyn! You made it!" Aaron said. She took her normal seat across from him.

"Yeah, I made it." Evelyn tried and failed to sound excited.

Caroline watched her suspiciously. Evelyn gave her a look back, silently begging her not to ask. Caroline shrugged and fiddled with her dice, but Evelyn knew better than to believe Caroline would let it go; she had simply resigned to ask later.

David turned on his computer and grabbed a tray of dice. "Let's get started."

Clarissa and Jareth burst into the inn, prepared to scold Jemma for her deception, but their team was nowhere to be found. They grabbed some drinks, sat down at an empty table, and cast a few messaging spells to summon their friends.

Jemma cheered with the crowd as Derek took a punch to the face. He was losing, but Jemma didn't care. Fun didn't require victory.

Derek froze suddenly and then sighed. In his moment of pause, he was knocked to the ground, conscious still but surrendering. She was confused until she heard Clarissa's voice in her head. 'Team meeting at the inn immediately.'

Elijah walked through the town with a bag full of supplies. He had gathered everything the group needed to travel back to Mistcoast. They had finished their quest, and it felt time to return home.

He missed his son. He could only imagine the mayhem Tobias was probably causing, running amok in the city. Elijah left the kid with his aunt, Elijah's sister, and made Tobias promise to obey everything she said, but he wasn't naive enough to believe the promises of an eight-year-old.

'We need you back at the inn for a team meeting. It's important.' Jareth's voice reeked of worry.

Elijah changed course and headed back to the inn. Tobias would have to wait.

"The good news is that we delivered the scrolls to Kinsley, and she paid us as promised," Clarissa said, distributing gold coins to her friends. Jareth didn't mirror her calm demeanor. He glared at Jemma, who refused to acknowledge him.

"The bad news is that we stole the scrolls," Clarissa continued. "They never belonged to Kinsley to begin with, which means we're probably wanted thieves in Illia."

"Then we don't return to Illia. We head back to Mistcoast," Elijah said. Clarissa nodded in agreement.

"But we have to return to Illia!" Jemma exclaimed.

"And why is that?" Jareth asked.

"We have to collect our payment for stealing the scrolls."

"From who?" Derek asked.

Jemma sighed in frustration. "From the thieves' guild!"

The table was suddenly quiet. "I thought you didn't work for them anymore," Elijah said calmly.

"This was just one time. I'm less like an employee and more like a contractor."

"You knew this whole time that we were stealing?" Derek asked.

"We all knew we were stealing something!" Jemma argued.

"We thought we were returning something to its rightful owner," Jareth said.

"What's the difference? Who gets to say who the rightful owner is? The thieves' guild may have been the ones behind this quest, but that doesn't make it any less legitimate. I even negotiated with the guild for them to pay us a sum too. The people that had those scrolls were from a rival guild called the Red Coin. They're not heroes. We stole from criminals." Jemma glared back at Jareth. "Yes, I lied to get you to agree to this quest. Get over it."

"If there's more payment waiting for us, we might as well go get it," Derek said. "We could all use the money."

"You're right," Elijah agreed. "We'll stop by Illia on the way to Mistcoast. We leave tomorrow. All of you, get some rest."

After a peaceful night of sleep, the group headed towards the sunrise. The walk abruptly reminded Clarissa of her wounded leg. The injury probably wasn't prepared for this length of journey, but there seemed to be no other choice.

She felt the tension in the group like a weight on her back. They were quiet—too quiet. They walked in silence in their typical marching order: Elijah leading, and Derek trailing behind. Long walks normally called for stories. Derek would tell an inflated tale about winning a fist fight, or Jareth would lecture them about the mechanics of spell-casting. Clarissa and Elijah liked to talk about their childhoods in Mistcoast. Jemma would start an impromptu show-and-tell with her latest "borrowed" treasures. Today, however, there were no stories to be told, no words to be spoken.

The silence was shattered by the high-pitched roaring of a creature in the sky. A shadow appeared from above, and a blue baby dragon fell in front of them. It whimpered in pain as blood poured from a wound on its wing. Derek approached cautiously, and the group froze in fearful anticipation, weapons ready for an attack. The dragon, however, didn't seem to mind the strange human nearing it. Derek inspected its injury. "It looks like a cut from a blade. Someone tried to kill it."

"It probably can't fly far with a wing like that," Clarissa said. She joined Derek's side and stood on her toes to pet the baby dragon on its head. "Do you think you can heal it?"

"It'll heal with time," Derek promised. The baby dragon licked his face.

Clarissa giggled. "It likes you."

Suddenly another roar came from above, this one louder, resonating around them. A larger shadow appeared. "Run!" Elijah screamed as an adult blue dragon flew towards them.

"We didn't hurt your baby! We were trying to help it!" Clarissa yelled. She wanted desperately to talk her way out of the fight. If she could simply convince the dragon not to kill her, then she wouldn't have to die. "I don't want to hurt you! Please don't hurt us."

To no one's surprise, the dragon didn't speak English.

It dove towards the party. Clarissa trailed behind, her injury impeding her sprinting skills. The dragon grabbed at her with its claw, piercing her shoulder and back with its talons. It dragged her into the air as it chased the rest of the party. An arrow flew towards her and pierced the scales right above Clarissa's head. The dragon shrieked and dropped Clarissa. The wind whipped at the free-falling girl, tossing her around like a toy, disrupting her sense of direction. She screamed, gaining momentum as the ground below grew closer.

Her vision went black as she slammed into the dirt.

Jareth cast a shield spell on Clarissa. A translucent force field surrounded her, blocking any further harm from coming her way. He refocused his attention on the dragon, casting spells to injure it as much as he could while still keeping up the shield to protect Clarissa. Derek shot arrow after arrow at the dragon until it finally fell to the ground. Elijah stabbed it with his sword, ending the fight only seconds after it began. With a shaky deep breath, he sheathed his sword and headed towards the force field.

"Clarissa!" Her eyes fluttered open to see shadowy figures outlined by the sun above. She blinked, trying to make out the people, but her vision didn't cooperate. That's when the pain set in. Her back ached, and her limbs refused to move. "Clarissa?" The voice spoke again, stating her name like a question.

"She's breathing." Another voice spoke this time.

"We have to keep moving. I don't feel like adding another day to our journey." It was the initial voice again.

"We can't leave her!" a girl called out.

"I didn't say that! Are you crazy? I wouldn't leave her." She felt an arm slide under her back, and another under her legs, before she was lifted off the ground.

Her vision betrayed her again as the blurry image faded to black.

Elijah carried the unconscious girl towards Illia, praying she would recover. Derek continually reassured him that her heartbeat and breathing were steady. He promised she would wake up soon, but Elijah found it hard to believe. Her eyes were closed and her body was limp. He turned to Jareth beside him. "I need you to teach her better self-defense spells."

"She wants to learn enchantment spells next," Jareth argued.

"I don't care. When we get to Illia, I'll take the others to get the gold, and you can give her another lecture on magic. Teach her a shield spell or teleportation or anything she can use to get away from the things trying to kill her. I'm not letting a member of this team die."

Jareth nodded. "I'll teach her."

Clarissa whimpered. Eli paused and set her in the grass as she awoke. Tears streamed down her face. "What happened?"

Jareth held her hand. "You're okay. I'm here. We're all here."

Her green eyes stared into his. "We're okay."

He brushed her blonde hair out of her face. "We're okay."

Clarissa held Jareth's hand as they continued their travels. It was comforting, knowing she wasn't alone. The group walked and camped and walked again and camped again. On the third day, they finally reached the small town of Illia.

"You almost killed me!" Evelyn yelled at David.

He laughed. "It was one dragon, and it was weak. You need to get better at dodging."

"The dice didn't want me to dodge. I rolled a one, and then a two, and then another one."

"Maybe you need new dice," Aaron said. "Yours are just unlucky."

Caroline nodded in agreement. "Stop playing with solid green dice. If you want better rolls, you need something more exciting. Did you know that sparkly dice roll higher numbers?"

"I don't think statistics care about glitter," Evelyn argued.

"Everything cares about glitter," Caroline said. "Let's go dice shopping tomorrow. I'll pick you up at six."

Evelyn looked at Oliver, then at Caroline. "Why is everyone adding events to my calendar without my consent?"

Caroline shrugged. "Why not?"

Evelyn rolled her eyes. "Fine. Tomorrow at six."

Monday, September 30

Evelyn walked into class four minutes early. Unsurprisingly, her professor had already started talking. He often treated the class duration as a suggestion.

"—six questions with an hour and a half time limit. I don't want to waste class time on tests anymore, so you'll be taking this one in the testing center. The test opens on Thursday at noon and closes Saturday at 8 p.m. Make sure you have an appointment scheduled with the testing center. You're allowed a calculator and scratch paper. Remember, the testing center does not allow—"

She tuned out his repetition of the testing center policies. Over the past four years, the rules had been ingrained in her memories time and time again. She opened the testing center website and raced the students beside her to get the most desirable test times.

Her laptop, of course, decided it was time for a software update. She stared at the blue screen and impatiently scrutinized the completion percentage. Several students around her closed their computers and opened their notebooks as the professor began working practice problems.

After ten minutes, her computer completed the unnecessary update. She re-navigated to the testing center website and logged in. The only option left was Saturday morning. She selected 9 a.m. and confirmed her testing appointment. Then she texted Mr. Alfred a long paragraph explaining why she couldn't make it to work on Saturday and apologizing profusely.

She put her phone away until class ended and checked for text messages on her way out. There was one: short and simple.

> *K. Good luck on the test.*

Evelyn focused on her breathing to keep herself calm as she walked across campus to book club. She dreaded the interaction with Erica, but she knew she couldn't avoid her forever. When she arrived at the library, Erica and Beckett were already sitting together in the busy room, whispering and laughing and holding hands. Melanie caught Evelyn's attention and gestured to the seat beside her.

"Did you read the chapter for this week?" Melanie asked.

Evelyn nodded. "I didn't really like it. Too much exposition."

"Agreed."

Silence filled the seconds that felt like minutes.

"How's your book going?" Evelyn asked.

"Good."

Silence returned, and tension flooded the space between them, creating an invisible barrier brought by their argument two weeks ago. Their conversation was uncomfortable, but the wall between them was even more so, until Evelyn dared to try to break it. "I think you were right."

"About what?" Melanie asked.

"Beckett."

Melanie sighed. "For Erica's sake, I wish I wasn't."

Evelyn hopped into the passenger seat of Caroline's car. After a long day of classes, homework, and poor attempts to write an essay, she was grateful for a break, even one somewhat forced upon her.

"So what was that weird look you had yesterday?" Caroline wasted no time before revealing the true reason for their shopping trip.

"It's... It's a long story," Evelyn said.

Caroline checked her watch. "I don't have to be at work for another 14 hours. We have all night, kiddo."

Evelyn sighed. "Can we get burgers? I haven't eaten anything today."

Caroline nodded. "Sweet potato fries make everything better."

They sat down at a table in the corner of the small, cramped restaurant. Caroline watched Evelyn, patiently waiting for her to explain her behavior. Finally, after finishing her burger and stuffing her mouth with fries, she was ready to talk.

"Oliver said something weird the other day."

Caroline laughed. "That's no surprise."

"No, it was weirder than normal." Evelyn paused. Oliver's words looped in her head but refused to leave her mouth. "He... well... we were at the boba shop."

"Working on your law school applications?"

Evelyn nodded. "Yes, and he started to leave, but he was acting... nice..."

"So? Oliver's a mess sometimes, but he's not a jerk."

Evelyn fidgeted nervously with a napkin. "Well... I... I asked him if our meeting for boba tea was a date."

Caroline rolled her eyes and laughed. "It wasn't a date, Evelyn. Oliver doesn't like you like that. You don't need to overthink it."

"I know it wasn't a date! He told me." Evelyn jumped to defensiveness.

"Then what's the problem?" Caroline asked.

Evelyn paused again, until finally, she was able to force the words out in a whisper. "He said that he wouldn't date his best friend's crush." The words spoken aloud were like a checkered flag, triggering a race of thoughts in her head.

Caroline shrugged. "I still don't see the problem."

Evelyn's eyes opened wide at Caroline's nonchalance. "It means one of the guys likes me! What am I supposed to do with that information?"

"Wait, is this new information to you?" Caroline laughed again.

"Yes! I don't even know which of the guys it is! It must be someone in the friend group, right? It's not David, because he likes you, and it's clearly not Oliver, so that leaves Aaron and Liam, and—"

"Evelyn, you really don't know who it is?" Caroline interrupted.

Evelyn shook her head. "How would I?"

"Because everyone else knows." Caroline took a sip of her drink. "You need to stop overthinking this. Let's go buy dice."

Evelyn's jaw dropped. "You know? Who is it?"

Caroline shook her head and held up her hands in surrender. "I'm not getting involved in this. You're oblivious sometimes, but you're not dumb. You'll figure it out."

Evelyn, in fact, did not figure it out. She stared out the window at the blurry passing landscape outside Caroline's car. She was a professional overthinker, and Caroline had handed her a perfect opportunity to practice her skills.

Clearly, it was Aaron or Liam. It had to be, right? Oliver had other friends that she had met a couple times, but none knew her too well. On top of that, Oliver didn't like these guys enough to call them his best friends. He had Evelyn, Caroline, David, Liam, and Aaron, and he didn't really care to meet people outside of the group.

Even if she figured out who liked her, what was she supposed to do with that knowledge? Should she ask them on a date? Did she want to date one of these guys? Did she want to date anyone at all? Dating was awkward and vulnerable and terrifying. It was the perfect opportunity for hurt and heartbreak. Why would she put herself through that? Why would anyone?

"Evelyn?" Caroline interrupted her internal dialogue. "We're here. Come on!" She jumped out of the car and practically ran towards the store. "What kind of dice do you want? Glitter? Gemstone? Metal?"

"I don't know." Evelyn struggled to pull her attention away from her inner dilemma.

"What's your favorite color?" Caroline asked.

"Green."

"That's a good start. What's your second favorite color?" Caroline continued interrogating Evelyn about her preferences. Evelyn answered every question without complaint. She needed something—anything—to think about other than men.

Tuesday, October 1

Evelyn left the on-campus coffee shop and headed towards the honors lounge. With her essay due Friday, test due Saturday, and law school applications due as soon as possible, she adopted her favorite study spots as her home for the week. She found her usual table and unpacked from her backpack everything she needed for the test. Textbooks, notebooks, and homework packets stacked in a pile over a foot tall. College math seemed to be a contributing factor to deforestation.

"What is that for?" Melanie asked, watching Evelyn build the precarious tower of books and papers.

"My test on Saturday."

"You have a test on a Saturday? That's horrible," Melanie said. "I'm guessing it's a math test, right? I wish I could help, but I barely passed college algebra."

"If it makes you feel better, I barely passed rhetoric. I hated that class." Evelyn paused. "Actually, there is one thing you could help me with."

Melanie shrugged. "I can try."

Evelyn opened a document on her computer. "This is my personal statement; It's supposed to explain why I want to go to law school. Do you think you can proofread it for me?" She set her computer in front of Melanie, waiting impatiently for Melanie to read.

Melanie read for a minute then sighed. "I can't edit while you're staring at me. Go study for your test. Give me half an hour."

Evelyn hesitantly walked away, leaving her laptop and poorly written statement in Melanie's hands. She distracted herself with math problems, resisting the urge to look over at Melanie every few seconds. Melanie stared at the laptop, focused, then left the room, returning with a stack of papers and a red pen. Evelyn took a deep breath and forced herself to focus on the equation in front of her.

After a small eternity, Melanie handed the stack of papers to Evelyn. It was her statement: printed out, double-spaced, and covered in red edits. "Your grammar is decent. Your punctuation needed some work, but it's okay; that's fixable. I like the story about your sister, but we need to work on the tone. You sound desperate."

"I am desperate," Evelyn said.

"Maybe you are, but this essay reads 'please, pretty please, let me into your fancy school.' It needs some self-confidence but not so much that it sounds arrogant. And you might need to improve your vocabulary. You want to sound well-educated without sounding like you used a thesaurus for every word. Also, work on your sentences. You want a variety of sentence structures: simple, compound, and complex, some short and some long. But you have a good start."

Evelyn rolled her eyes. "Thanks." Her tone reeked of sarcasm, and she sighed at her own stupidity. "I'm sorry. I really am grateful for your help. I'm just stressed by how many things I need to balance in this essay."

Melanie shrugged. "Welcome to being a writer."

Wednesday, October 2

Evelyn sat alone at a table in the library. She worked on her personal statement between bites of food but made little improvement. The essay read like a list of facts instead of a carefully woven narrative. Her writing style was passable in a research paper, but failed miserably at convincing someone she should be allowed to attend law school. She was thankful, however, for the quiet corner of the library giving her a place to work alone in peace. Between

Caroline, Melanie, study groups, and classes, she felt as though she hadn't had a moment to herself all week.

"Evelyn?" She heard her name called from behind and sighed at the interruption to the silence she had been so grateful for. Rowan sat at the table across from her. "Have you seen Erica?"

Evelyn shook her head. "I think your little sister hates me now. We got into a fight last week."

"What happened?" Rowan asked.

Evelyn recapped the argument for him: Erica described the date, the girls talked about Erica and Beckett's first kiss, and Erica became angry at Evelyn for questioning her relationship. "Maybe I was too harsh. I'm just worried about her. She's so young and naive, and I don't want her to get hurt."

Rowan nodded. "Trust me, I understand. She always sees the best in people, but sometimes it blinds her from seeing the worst."

"Maybe I was overthinking it, though," Evelyn said. "Maybe Beckett is a great guy."

"Have you met Beckett?" Rowan asked with a laugh.

"A few times," Evelyn said. "He's in our book club."

Rowan shook his head. "I met him the other day when he came to pick up Erica. He's an idiot. I told her to break up with him."

Evelyn's eyes widened. "You did? How did that go?"

"How do you think it went?" Rowan said. "She screamed at me from across the living room and threw a pillow at me.

She said I was being an overprotective jerk, just like Beckett said I'd be." He added finger quotes around the last phrase.

Evelyn rolled her eyes. "Beckett also told her that Melanie is an insecure liar. I'd love to hear what he has to say about me."

"Well, he said that anyone who isn't supportive of their relationship is a bad friend." Rowan gave a laugh that Evelyn didn't reciprocate. Her head dropped to look down at her feet. He nudged her arm. "Hey, don't let that get to you. Beckett doesn't get to define your character."

"You're right," Evelyn said, but her confidence disagreed. What if Beckett was right? What if she really was a terrible friend?

Rowan glanced at the time on his phone. "I need to go find my sister. I'll see you around!" He wandered off into the library.

She closed the essay and opened the webpage to check for recently added grades. She had barely passed her topology homework and had failed her psychology quiz. There was a newly uploaded ten-page document detailing the statistics course final project despite the fact that they hadn't completed the midterm yet.

Professors really knew how to make a bad day worse.

Evelyn plugged in her earbuds as she walked home in the evening, listening to a true crime podcast. She watched video game live streams as she cooked herself pasta for dinner. Once the live stream ended, she binged her favorite childhood show until she fell asleep and let her mind fill with dreams. There was not a second of silence, for silence allowed for thoughts which forced Evelyn to face the truth. Distraction was better, simpler, easier than confronting the frustrations and failures in front of her. Unfortunately, inevitably, her dreams would end, and reality would come back into view.

Thursday, October 3

Evelyn dragged the grocery bags into her dorm, determined to carry them in all one trip. Grocery shopping was slowly becoming her most dreaded chore. Her arms gave out the moment she entered her dorm. The bags slammed into the tile and food scattered across the kitchen floor. She picked up a box of pasta and a couple cans of soup and shoved them into the crowded pantry.

"I failed my calculus test." The voice echoed through the seemingly empty room. It took Evelyn a minute to notice her blanket-wrapped roommate curled up on the couch like a burrito.

"I can help you study for your next one," Evelyn offered.

Sobs escaped from the blanket on the couch. "It's useless. I'm bad at math."

Evelyn pulled at the blanket, revealing Bethany's tear-filled eyes. "I'm bad at writing," Evelyn said, "but I've learned a thing or two this week. If I can learn to write, I'm sure you can learn math."

"Not even blueberry muffins could save me from the evils of calculus," Bethany cried. She wiped the tears off her cheek with the blanket. "Thank you for helping me bake muffins, by the way. It meant a lot."

"Do you want me to help you study for your next test?" Evelyn asked.

Bethany nodded. "Can you help me bake more muffins, too?"

Evelyn hugged her. "Of course."

Friday, October 4

Avery:

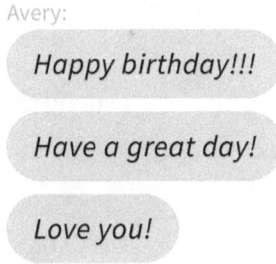

Happy birthday!!!

Have a great day!

Love you!

Evelyn glanced at her calendar. Her sister was right—it was her birthday, and she had totally forgotten. It didn't matter anyways. Life, much less college, didn't pause for birthdays.

She parked her car and headed inside. Unlike last week, she could study in peace, without interruptions from Oliver and law school applications. She thrived on routine: driving to the same boba shop, saying hi to Piper, ordering the same tea, and sitting at the same table. She walked inside the door and immediately paused.

The girl behind the register sat in a chair with her feet propped up on the counter. Her long black hair hid her face. She held her phone in her lap, playing a video that drowned out the soft piano music on the cafe speakers. She hadn't even noticed a customer walk in.

Evelyn approached, walking louder than necessary to get her attention without words. The girl still didn't notice. "Can I get a strawberry green tea?" Evelyn asked.

The girl sighed and pushed her hair out of her face, propping her phone up against the register. "Fine. Do you want boba too?"

"Crystal boba. Where's Piper?"

The girl rolled her eyes. "Piper's gone. I fired her." She slammed the cup on the counter and poured in green tea.

"Why'd you fire her?" Evelyn asked.

The girl shrugged. "She was annoying. I didn't like her. Why do you care? Are you her friend or something?"

"Kind of."

The girl set Evelyn's drink on the counter and returned her attention to the video on her phone.

Evelyn left, determined to find a new study spot for today and a new boba shop for next week.

As Evelyn drove, her phone exploded with notifications from the group chat.

Caroline:

> *Happy birthday Evelyn!*

Liam:

> *happy birthday!*

Oliver:

> *party tonight?*

Aaron:

> *I like parties!*

Caroline:

> *Party at David's house!*

Evelyn:

> *I have to study for my test tomorrow, and I have an essay due at midnight :(but I'll see you idiots Sunday*

Oliver:

> *who puts a test on a saturday?*

Evelyn:

> *Math professors. They hate us.*

Aaron:

Test prep is a horrible birthday present

After wandering campus for half an hour, Evelyn finally found an empty whiteboard in a quiet spot in the basement of the library. She claimed a table and dumped out her heavy backpack of class notes, then turned off her phone and hid it in the bottom of her now-empty bag. She couldn't afford distractions today.

She started with the AI essay. To her surprise, with Melanie's tips from the week prior, the assignment wasn't too difficult. Her bullet points of research quickly become a ten-page paper about the applications of artificial intelligence for paralegals and lawyers. She proofread for errors and submitted the essay online. Then she moved on to the task she truly dreaded.

Slowly but surely, she filled the whiteboard with theorems and formulas and color-coded examples. Partial differential equations was becoming the bane of her existence. The class only lasted sixteen weeks, but it felt like an eternity. It was hard—unnecessarily hard—and she despised the professor who refused to acknowledge that students have other responsibilities outside his class. She fueled her anger and frustration at the problem on the whiteboard until finally, miraculously, she solved it. She continued, solving two, then three, then ten, until the board was filled with a rainbow of writing, an array of problems each in a different hue. She sat down. Now she just needed to memorize every process on the board.

She had promised herself she'd keep her phone hidden away, but she needed to use the camera to immortalize the temporary dry-erase writing. She turned on the screen to see a missed call from her mom and a single text from Liam sent in a private chat instead of the group.

Liam:

> *do you want a break from studying? i have a birthday cupcake for you. i can bring it to your study spot so you don't have to waste too much time.*

She looked at the wall of writing and smiled at her progress. Math was hard. She deserved a cupcake.

Liam met her in the library basement 20 minutes later, holding a dessert in each hand. "Two red velvet cupcakes!"

Evelyn smiled. "Did you know red velvet is my favorite?"

"That's why I brought them." He handed her a cupcake, and they sat down at the table in the now-empty library basement. It was eerily quiet this time of night, but Evelyn enjoyed the peacefulness.

"How is studying going?" Liam asked.

She shrugged. "It's going well, I think. I finished the essay." She took a bite. "These are good!" she said through a mouthful of cake. "Where did you buy these?"

He smiled. "I made them. This was my first attempt. I'm honestly shocked they turned out edible."

"The icing looked so good, too!" she said.

He laughed. "Only on these two. The other ten were a total disaster."

"You only made a dozen?" she asked. "I figured you'd make a bunch for game night tomorrow."

"I thought maybe you'd like something calmer, so I ditched the party idea for cupcakes in the library." Liam looked at her nervously. "Was I wrong? I can still plan a party for Sunday. I have plenty of time. I could—"

"No, Liam, this is perfect." She smiled, and he smiled back, staring into her green eyes. She wondered how she'd never noticed the way he looked at her: like a princess, a treasure, a dream. He looked at her the way people looked at sunsets, watching beauty in its natural form. He smiled at her the way adults smiled at children and children smiled at trinkets from the treasure box at school.

"Oh, good," he said with relief. "If you hated it, I was going to tell you it was all Caroline's idea, or maybe we would just have to call you princess again." He laughed with her like an old friend, like they'd known each other for years, and he teased her like family, knowing exactly how much taunting she could handle.

He knew her: her overthinking, her anxiety, her stubbornness, her terrible video game skills. He knew the way she hated four-sided dice and books about love and everything at the school cafeteria. He knew when she was scared and when she was stressed, when she needed a hug and when she needed a distraction. He knew her habits, her routines, the way she packed her dice neatly in order, the way she braided her hair when she hadn't washed it and played with it when she was nervous.

Her fingers fidgeted with a lock of blonde hair. "Thanks for bringing me a cupcake. I should get back to studying soon."

He stood from his chair. "Happy birthday, Evie." She watched him walk away up the library stairs, leaving her alone again with her math and her thoughts.

Caroline ✦

OCT 13, 10:52 AM

How did your test go???

I aced it, I think

It's Liam, right?

What's Liam?

Oliver's best friend with a crush.

Of course it's Liam

What am I supposed to do?

I don't know...

Enter your message...

6

Sunday, October 6

Illia was quiet after dark. Only a tiny ray of sun peeked over the horizon. There were a few people walking home and a few others lurking in the shadows, but for the most part, the streets were empty and the oil lamps were dark. The silence magnified every sound: every footstep, every heartbeat. Clarissa squeezed Jareth's hand tight, as if he could protect her from the darkness.

Jemma skipped down the sidewalk, humming a repetitive melody. She froze in front of a small building. "It's here!" she whispered. "The guild is in the basement. This is where we get paid."

Elijah turned to Jareth. "Take Clarissa to set up camp and work on those spells I mentioned. We'll take care of this." He took a deep breath and walked into the building with an air of confidence, as if he belonged there, as if he was in charge.

Clarissa turned to Jareth. "What spells was he talking about?"

"Let's find a place to camp, and I'll explain." He led her away from the building.

Elijah followed Jemma's instructions perfectly: walk to the door behind the stairs, knock seven times, pause, then knock twice more and state his name. Slowly, the door peeked open and a young boy stuck his head out. He was barely tall enough for his hair to brush against the doorknob. "I've never heard of you, Elijah Praetor."

"Hey, Scraps!" Jemma waved at him.

"Jemma! Hey! Did you bring me anything this time?"

She held out an apple and a cup. Scraps threw open the door and took both the items.

"Does that cup belong to the inn in Caridelle?" Elijah asked.

"Now it belongs to Scraps in Illia!" Jemma walked through the door. "Where's the boss guy? I want to get paid."

"The boss guy? Did you forget his name?" Scraps asked.

Jemma shrugged. "After the third one died, I stopped memorizing the names."

"The new guy goes by Artemis. I'll take you to him." Scraps led them through a large room, scattered with tables, only half of which sat upright. There were mugs and bowls and plates, some intact and others shattered into tiny pieces on the floor. "Sorry for the mess. There was a party last night: a baby shower for Lila."

"Since when does a thieves' guild host baby showers?" Derek mumbled under his breath.

Jemma glared at him. "Are you judging us?"

"Us? I thought you left this place," Elijah said.

Jemma shrugged. "I did. Mostly."

Scraps pushed open the door to a small room with a couch, a coffee table, and a few chairs. He ushered them inside and slammed the door closed. Artemis sat relaxed on the couch with his black boots propped on the coffee table. His disheveled black hair barely brushed the collar of his worn leather jacket. He grinned at the trio as they entered. "Jemma! It's nice to see you. These must be your friends."

"I'm Elijah, and this is Derek." Eli sat down in one of the chairs. "You must be Artemis."

"That's me! I'm hoping you're here to tell me about the success of the little task we gave you."

"Precisely. We stole the scrolls from the Red Coin and gave them to Kinsley. Jemma said you had payment for us."

"Of course! But how do I know I can trust you, Elijah Praetor?" Artemis propped his feet up on the coffee table.

"If you didn't trust Jemma, you wouldn't have given her this task," Elijah said.

Artemis nodded. "That's true. Jemma, did you steal the scrolls and give them to Kinsley?"

"Eli and Jareth stole them, and Clarissa and Jareth gave them to Kinsley. I fought some wolves and a dragon. Derek healed everybody. It was a team effort."

"But did you see the scrolls handed to Kinsley?" Artemis asked.

She shook her head. "No."

"And you two didn't either?" Artemis asked.

Elijah and Derek both shook their heads.

Artemis sighed. "You're not asking me to trust you. You're asking me to trust your friends, whom I've never met. Why weren't they the ones to come here?"

"Clarissa is badly injured from the dragon, and Jareth is taking care of her," Elijah argued.

"It sounds like Derek is your healer. Why isn't he with her?"

"It's complicated," Elijah said.

"It doesn't have to be. Just send a quick message and tell them to come here." Artemis watched, waiting. Elijah sighed. "None of you know the message spell?" Artemis asked.

"Jareth and Clarissa are the spellcasters," Elijah explained.

"Then you'd better go find them. I'll wait here. Once I hear directly from an eyewitness that the scrolls were given to Kinsley, I'll pay what was promised." He snapped his fingers, and the door swung open.

Jareth stopped in a clearing on the outskirts of town. "This should work." He unpacked a tent and started setting up camp.

"What did Elijah mean when he said I needed to work on spells?" Clarissa asked again.

Jareth set down the tent poles. "I need to teach you the shield spell. I don't want you getting hurt in every fight."

Clarissa rolled her eyes. "Jareth, I know I'm weak, but—"

"You are not weak." Jareth glared at her. "You are the most valuable member of this team. I can't afford to lose you, Claire." His glare faded into a soft look of concern. "Please, can I teach you the spell?"

His kindness melted her cold stubbornness. Her shoulder relaxed. "Okay."

He held out his hands. "Follow my lead. We'll practice as long as it takes."

Elijah, Jemma, and Derek wandered the town aimlessly. "We're never going to find them," Jemma complained. The group was left with two time-consuming options: wait for a message spell that they could respond to or search the whole area until they stumbled upon Jareth and Clarissa.

"Do you think if we just yell really loudly, they'll hear us?" Derek asked.

"There's a slight chance they'll hear us and a definite chance we'll wake up this entire street," Eli said. "People don't like being woken up, and I don't feel like making enemies."

"What if we split the party again to cover more ground?" Derek joked. "Splitting the party went so well the first time."

"Okay!" Jemma ran off.

"Jemma, no!" Elijah yelled. He turned to grab her arm, but it was too late. She was gone, absorbed by the shadows of the night.

After hours of practice, Clarissa finally cast the shield spell. It would take many more hours to master the spell and cast it consistently, but at least there was a small chance it worked in the case of an emergency. Jareth smiled. "Good job."

"Thanks." She looked around at the tents he had set up while she practiced. "We should get some sleep soon. Where are the others?"

"I'll send them a message." Jareth cast the spell to talk to Elijah. 'We set up camp on the north side of town. Where are you?'

'Looking for you,' Eli responded. 'Meet us at the point where we split up.'

"Thank goodness we found you," Elijah said as Jareth and Clarissa approached. "We need you to go talk to Artemis."

"Who's Artemis?" Clarissa asked.

"The leader of the thieves' guild. He won't give us the money unless he gets to talk to you two."

"That's fine; I'll talk to him," Clarissa said. "Where's Jemma?"

"We don't know," Elijah said.

Clarissa sighed. "You lost her again?"

"She ran off!" Derek said.

Jareth sent her a message, but as expected, received no response. Clarissa headed into the building to talk with Artemis. "We'll find her later."

Clarissa sat down in the chair across from Artemis. Jareth stood beside her, his hand on her shoulder. Artemis seemed calm and certain, but Clarissa saw through the act. His eyes, mostly hidden behind his messy hair, revealed his apprehension. "You wanted to talk to us," Clarissa said.

Artemis nodded. He made a gesture with his hands, and silver magic surrounded them like a fog that dissipated in seconds.

"What was that?" Clarissa whispered with concern.

"A truth spell," Jareth said. Clarissa could hear his eyes roll in his tone.

Artemis nodded. "A truth spell, indeed. Did you two deliver the scrolls to Kinsley?"

They both nodded. "I handed them directly to her," Jareth promised.

"And Kinsley was satisfied with the delivery?" he asked.

"Jareth irritated her a little," Clarissa said. "I kicked him out and had a good little talk with her. We're friends now."

Artemis laughed. "That's no surprise. Kinsley is particular with who she calls friend. She's much better at collecting enemies." He pulled out a small pouch of coins from his jacket and handed it to Clarissa. "Good luck in your adventures."

Jemma was walking down the alley, hiding in the shadows, when she suddenly paused. Someone was following her. She could have sworn she heard footsteps and a high-pitched giggle. She walked back to the entrance of the alley and peaked around the corner. Scraps smiled at her.

"Scraps! You scared me!"

"I'm sorry! I just wanted to see what you were doing."

"I'm just looking for my friends," she said. "Seriously, you scared me. I thought someone from the Red Coin might have followed—"

"Roll for agility."

Caroline glared at David. "Oh, no."

"Roll for agility," he repeated.

She tossed the dice in the middle of the table. It landed on one. She gasped.

A grin slowly spread across David's face. "You hear the thud of boots approaching from behind. Before you can react, your vision goes dark."

"David!" Caroline yelled across the table. "You can't end the game with me getting kidnapped!"

He smiled. "That's what happens when you split the party."

"It was Aaron's idea!" Caroline said.

"It was a joke!" Aaron argued.

"This is not good." Evelyn laid her head on the table, face down, eyes staring at the grain of the wood an inch away. "We're all going to die."

Aaron, David, and Oliver headed towards the living room, debating the pros and cons of splitting the party. The only pro seemed to be chaos, but apparently that outweighed all the cons.

Liam moved to sit beside Evelyn. "How'd your test go?"

Her eyes widened. She was suddenly grateful for the table and long blonde hair hiding her face. Her heart pounded. Her conversation skills disappeared into an ocean of thoughts.

"Good." She settled on a simple one-word answer.

He laughed. "Are you going to keep your face against the table? I recommend sitting up and breathing."

She sat up, and her hair fell in her face, covering her eyes.

Liam laughed. "You're a mess, Evelyn." He stood up again and started packing leftovers to stash in the fridge.

Evelyn pushed her hair out of her face and turned to Caroline as Liam carried food out of the room.

"Did you hear him? I'm a mess," Evelyn said.

Caroline rolled her eyes. "He calls me a mess all the time, Evelyn. You're overthinking again."

Evelyn put her head back on the table. "I think he hates me."

Monday, October 7

If Evelyn was in charge of the world, math would never be taught before lunch. She sat in the back of her morning class, her brain fighting to keep her eyes open and her hand struggling to keep up with the professor in her messy notes. As class ended, she looked down at the scribbles. Her tilted writing on the notebook paper made the ruled lines look like only suggestions.

"By the way, your test scores should be released... now," the professor said as the clock hit 9:45. Everyone scrambled to navigate the app and check their grades.

Evelyn clicked to see her test grade: 80. Then she opened the syllabus and took out her calculator. Her 92.1

average on the concept quizzes and her 85.3 average on the pop quizzes were each worth 15%. The attendance was worth 10% and she had missed one day, and the tests and homework were worth equal amounts. Given her 93.2 homework average, and assuming her homework and quiz grades stayed the same, she needed an average of a 90.1 on the next two tests to make an A in the class.

She sighed in frustration. She couldn't afford another 80 on a test.

She tossed her laptop and calculator into her backpack and headed towards the library, pop music blaring through her headphones. Campus was always busy, but there was something strangely peaceful about the walk. Students were clustered together, some talking, some laughing, some crying probably over midterms. Squirrels chased each other across the grass, unafraid of the humans invading their space. A group of skateboarders flew recklessly through the crowds. Tables on the sidewalk were set up by student organizations and manned by members trying to persuade people to their cause. She passed old worn-down buildings next to brand new shiny ones, spaces overflowing with students and bike racks overflowing as well, benches and trees and flowers and bugs.

It was pure chaos, and Evelyn loved it.

The library was relatively quiet but equally hectic. There were tables full of backpacks and books and whiteboards full of diagrams and formulas. Evelyn walked past the crowds to the small classroom used for book club. The room was fairly empty, with only a few students mulling around. Erica sat in the back, reading a book.

Evelyn took a deep breath. She couldn't avoid her friend forever. She sat in the chair across from Erica. "How are you doing?"

Erica stared at her book, refusing to look at Evelyn. "Beckett told me not to talk to you."

"Seriously?" Evelyn watched, waiting for any reaction, but Erica refused to acknowledge her. She flipped to the next page of her book, paused, then flipped another page, stubbornly keeping her eyes and her focus on the novel. Finally, Evelyn stood up and walked away.

Melanie leaned against the wall, watching. "What was that?"

She sighed. "Erica won't talk to me."

"I'm sorry, Evelyn."

Beckett walked into the room and straight towards Erica. Her face lit up, and she set aside her book to hug him. He ran his fingers through her hair and kissed her on the cheek.

"I worry about her," Evelyn said.

Melanie nodded. "Me too."

Book club started. Beckett recommended students split up into smaller circles and immediately claimed Erica and his friends as a group of their own. Evelyn and Melanie joined a few other students to discuss the fantasy book. "Do you think he recommended smaller groups just to keep Erica away from us?" Evelyn whispered to Melanie.

Melanie sighed. "I'm sure of it."

After a long group discussion about world-building and magic systems, Evelyn and Melanie headed out of the library together. "How's your personal statement going?" Melanie asked.

Evelyn shrugged. "I made some of the edits you suggested, but it still feels mediocre."

"Do you want some help with it tomorrow? I had an idea that might help."

"Thanks. Let's meet up in the honors lounge."

Melanie handed Evelyn her phone. "Can I have your number? I'll figure out my plan for tomorrow and text you. I'm trying to schedule meetings with some of my beta readers, but coordinating is hard."

Evelyn typed in her phone number. "I've been reading your manuscript, by the way. I really like it. The magic, the mystery, the politics... it's great, honestly. I get so caught up in the story that I forget to make edits."

Melanie gave an obligatory smile. "Thanks."

"I'm serious. It's fantastic."

Her smile widened. "You really think so?"

Evelyn nodded. "I wouldn't lie to you."

Evelyn's next two classes were as equally boring as the first. She started the long walk to her dorm across campus, taking out her phone to connect her bluetooth earbuds only to notice a missed text from Caroline.

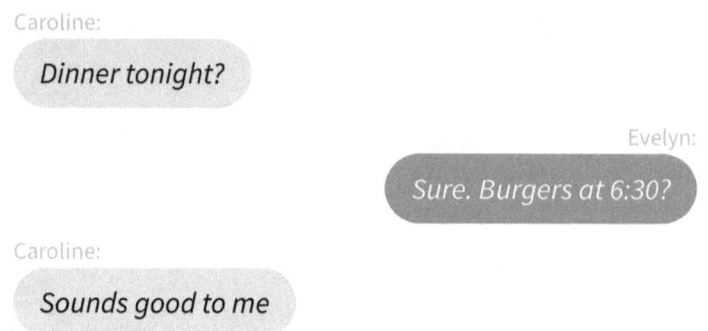

Evelyn tucked her phone back in her pocket. She felt guilty for her selfish motivations for dinner with Caroline. Someone needed to talk her through this Liam mess, and it clearly wasn't going to be Erica.

She honestly didn't know what to think. She had always enjoyed Liam's company. He was kind, relatable, patient, honest but gentle. Evelyn and Liam were close friends from the moment Aaron introduced them in the student union. They had a shared interest in math, strategy games, and late night walks around campus, although Evelyn never quite understood his desire to be an accountant. It sounded dreadfully boring to her, but she loved seeing the smile on his face every time he passed a CPA exam. His smile was contagious; she couldn't help but smile back, which only made him smile more, triggering a recursive cycle of joy. Still, she'd only ever thought of him as a friend. As she pondered that idea, she realized she'd really never thought of anyone as more than a friend since her date with Alex freshman year. She always told the story nonchalantly, as if it was one date and then they merely decided to go separate ways. It wasn't a lie, but it wasn't the full story. From Alex's perspective, that was exactly what happened, a first date that simply didn't lead to a second. Alex didn't know that Evelyn cried for hours that day. The tears weren't about Alex; they were about the rejection. It planted a narrative in her head that she would never be good enough. She considered herself perfectly average in every way: an average girl with average looks and average flirting skills. She had an average personality and average hobbies. Just like everyone around her, she was an average college student with an average course load and an average student loan balance. The only aspects of her life that she considered interesting weren't even hers: Clarissa could befriend anyone, Rose Thorn could decimate enemies, and the Scarlet Rebellion could overthrow monarchies. Evelyn was average and boring, and anyone reasonable wanted to date someone special. She was the type of girl who didn't get second dates, so what was the point of dating at all? It was an invitation for heartbreak and a magnet for hurt.

After a couple hours of mindless homework and racing thoughts, she headed to the burger restaurant. Caroline had beaten her there and ordered food for the both of them. "How was your day?" Caroline asked as Evelyn sat down across from her.

She stuffed her mouth with sweet potato fries and shrugged.

"My day was boring," Caroline said. "How were your classes?"

"Also boring," Evelyn said. "I have a question."

"Is it about Liam?"

"How'd you know?"

Caroline shrugged. "I'm basically a mind reader."

"What should I do?"

"Well, that depends," Caroline said. "Do you like him?"

"It doesn't really matter."

"Why not?"

Evelyn shrugged and shoveled another handful of fries into her mouth.

"Is this about Alex?" Caroline asked.

Evelyn shook her head. "I'm the kind of girl guys go on dates with when they're bored. I'm not the kind of girl they fall in love with and marry."

"Clearly Liam disagrees."

Evelyn shook her head again, trying and failing to convince herself that Caroline was wrong.

"Listen," Caroline continued, "Liam is far from superficial, and he knows you well. If he likes you, he has a good reason."

Evelyn wanted to argue, but she couldn't find a witty comeback. Caroline's logic was solid. "Then tell me what I'm supposed to do."

"I don't know, kiddo. I asked David last night, but he insists you should do nothing. He won't tell me why." She took a bite of her burger.

"Do you think Liam talked to David about me?"

"Definitely."

"Do you think he talked to all the guys?"

Caroline shook her head. "Probably just David. Trust me, Oliver and Aaron don't give great dating advice. David's pretty good at it."

"Of course you would say that."

She smiled. "I'm not much of a romantic, but David's great. Dating him was probably one of the best decisions I've ever made."

"Dating is terrifying. Skydiving sounds less risky."

Caroline laughed. "Are you really that scared to date anyone?"

"Of course I am!"

"Evelyn, life is full of risk. Every time you drive a car, there's a chance of crashing. Every time you take a test, there's a chance of failing. Every time you make a friend, there's a chance of betrayal. Every time you date, there's a chance of breaking up or cheating or emotional manipulation—"

"You're not making it sound appealing."

"—but it's worth it," Caroline said. "It's worth it because there's a chance of meeting the person you want to spend the rest of your life with." Caroline grinned the way she did when Jemma invented a scheme. "And then I get to help plan your wedding and be your maid of honor."

Evelyn laughed. "Wait, who said you'd be my maid of honor?"

"Well, you'd definitely be my maid of honor," Caroline said.

"Thanks." Evelyn took a deep breath. "It's still scary."

Caroline nodded. "Of course it is. That's normal. Being nervous means that you care."

"You give really good advice, Caroline."

She shrugged. "You're welcome."

Tuesday, October 8

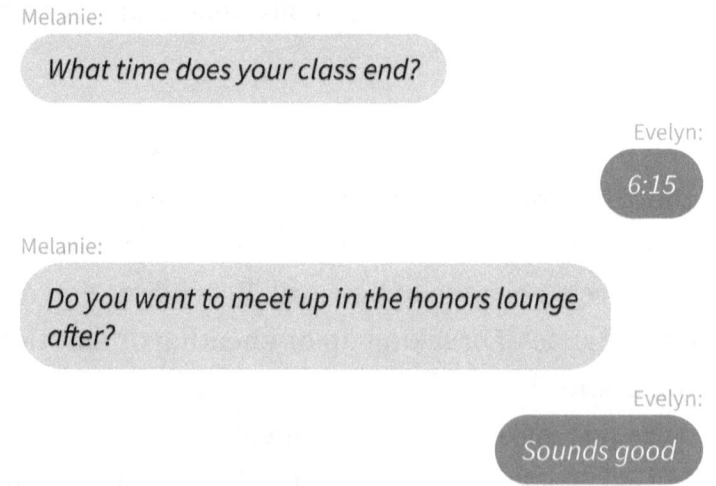

Melanie:
What time does your class end?

Evelyn:
6:15

Melanie:
Do you want to meet up in the honors lounge after?

Evelyn:
Sounds good

Evelyn walked into the chaos of the honors lounge, looking around for her newfound friend. Melanie was sitting on the couch in the corner, typing on her laptop. She closed it as soon as she noticed Evelyn. "Come, sit down. I have an idea." She opened her phone, tapped a few buttons, and set it on the arm of the couch.

Evelyn sat on the other end of the couch. "What's your genius idea?"

She smiled. "Tell me what's in your personal statement."

Evelyn watched her through squinted eyes. "You already read it. Why do you need me to tell you?"

"Just tell me."

Evelyn took out the printed copy covered in Melanie's red pen scribbles. "When I was 12 years old..." She began reading the essay out loud.

"No, don't read it to me." Melanie took the paper out of her hand. "Tell me the story. Tell me why you want to go to law school. Talk to me like a friend."

"Ok." Evelyn didn't understand the point, but she followed the instructions. "One time, when I was 12 years old and my sister was 6, we were eating breakfast together before school. My sister Avery opened a fresh box of her favorite cereal: Happy Hearts. The cereal was made of tiny hearts in a bunch of different colors: red, pink, purple, blue, and maybe some others. My sister's favorites were the blue ones. She said they tasted the best, like blueberries, her favorite fruit. She always picked them out of the bowl and saved them for last. But one day, she opened a new box of cereal, and there were no blue hearts. She was so angry. She started screaming and yelling. I tried calming her down, but it's hard to calm a raging six-year-old."

Melanie laughed. "So what did you do next?"

"My mom was out of the room, but she had left her phone, so I stole it and searched online. It turned out that the cereal company had stopped making the blue hearts. My sister didn't take that as an answer. She was so mad at the company for removing the best flavor."

"Did you ever figure out why they took out the blue ones?" Melanie asked.

"I looked it up a few years later to get the full story. Apparently, they took the blue out because it didn't match the color scheme. I guess they wanted the cereal to be more aesthetic or something like that." Evelyn laughed so hard that she struggled to continue the story. "The funniest part is that they never tasted different. The blue ones were the exact same recipe as all the others. They never tasted like blueberries at all."

"How does this relate to you becoming a lawyer?" Melanie asked.

"You read my statement. You already know this."

"Tell me anyways," Melanie insisted.

Evelyn sighed. "In Avery's little fit, she declared that we needed to sue that cereal company for taking out the blue hearts. I think she'd been watching too much of my mom's lawyer drama show on TV. I told her we couldn't sue a company for changing their cereal, but she didn't care. She kept screaming, calling it a 'huge mistake' and a 'kiss race to society.'"

"A 'kiss race'?" Melanie asked.

"I'm pretty sure she meant 'disgrace,'" Evelyn said. "She was so angry about the so-called injustice. When I told her we couldn't sue them, she asked why. I told her I'm not a lawyer, and that even if I was, I wouldn't win that lawsuit. She told me that I needed to become the 'bestest lawyer in the world'. I told her she was being stupid. But as I got older, I started learning about all the real injustices in the world, and I thought that maybe my little sister was right. Maybe I really could help people as a lawyer: not dumb kids with bad cereal, but people with real problems. I'm not some sort of hero or anything like that. I'm not going to save the world. I'm just hoping that, one case at a time, I can help people."

Melanie picked up her phone, and Evelyn's phone pinged with a new message. There was a voice recording. "That's a good story, Evelyn, but when you wrote it on paper, you were too busy trying to sound smart. Focus on sounding relatable. We want the reader to notice your personality, not only your intelligence. Listen to the recording and type all the words, then edit from there. It might take a while to type them all but you'll get it."

"You know your phone can automatically turn audio into text, right?" Evelyn asked.

Melanie gasped. "No way! I've been typing out my voice recordings of book ideas this whole time! It takes hours!"

Evelyn rolled her eyes. "Here, I'll show you." She took Melanie's phone and walked her through the steps.

"You're an absolute genius," Melanie said.

"My entire future depends on one essay and I can't write it. I wouldn't call myself a genius."

"You're still smarter than me. I have the IQ of a potato."

Evelyn laughed. She looked around the honors lounge, full of students, busy with activities, from studying to playing video games to building card towers. It was meant to be a gathering of the brightest students of the college. Instead, it attracted young optimistic freshmen who were destined to become hopeless pessimistic seniors, their hopes and dreams crushed by reality. Evelyn felt right at home.

Evelyn's mind ran wild as she sat in her apartment that night. For once, she almost wished for an essay or a project to focus her thoughts and energy. She paced around her room, annoyed with her test grade, nervous about Liam, and stressed about her law school applications. Finally, in her spiral of thoughts, she thought of an escape. She grabbed her backpack and pulled out Melanie's manuscript, along with her notes about the main character Adelaide, the rising tension of the plot, and the questions left unanswered. She opened to the last page she read, took a deep breath, and continued reading, letting Adelaide's problems overshadow her own.

Thursday, October 10

Evelyn's phone buzzed with a text from Caroline outside of the normal chat, starting a new group with Oliver missing.

Caroline:

David and I had the most genius idea!

Who wants to go to a middle school football game tonight???

Evelyn:

Are Oliver's kids playing?

Aaron:

Oliver has kids?? Wait until he finds out...

Evelyn:

I meant Oliver's students, idiot

Caroline:

Of course. That's why we're going. Wanna join?

Aaron:

I'm in!

Liam:

me too.

Evelyn:

Sure, I'll come

Caroline:

We'll meet at David's house and carpool.

It wasn't until Evelyn was halfway to David's house that she realized the evening would require interacting with Liam, preferably without making a fool of herself. She walked in the front door. David never bothered to lock it, so she never bothered to knock. "You made it!" Caroline hugged her as she entered the living room.

"Hey, Evelyn!" Liam waved at her from the kitchen. He acted so normal, like nothing had changed between them. Evelyn wasn't sure why his behavior surprised her. He didn't know that she had discovered that he liked her. Why would he act any differently?

She stepped towards the kitchen and waved back. "Hey, Liam!" She hid her overwhelm behind a friendly smile.

Before they had a chance to chat, David and Aaron headed towards the door. "Do we have everyone? Are you ready to go?" David asked Caroline.

Caroline nodded. "To the football game!"

Evelyn had always thought the football games on TV were slow, repetitive, and confusing. Middle school football was the exact same, except there were no commercials to interrupt the monotony.

Oliver didn't notice his friends enter the stadium. He was too focused on the students and their warm-ups. The group claimed an empty row of seats in the bleachers, joining tired parents and impatient siblings. Oliver's team—the Eagles—won the coin toss. Caroline cheered on the team full of kids she'd never met.

David laughed. "Caroline, it's a coin toss. They haven't even scored any points yet."

Caroline rolled her eyes. "Whatever it was, they won it!"

"You're not going to cheer them on for winning a game of chance?" Liam teased Evelyn.

She laughed and shook her head. "I prefer games of skill," she said as Oliver's team kicked the ball. A boy from the opposing team caught it, but one of the Eagles quickly tackled him. Everyone cheered.

"Does that count as skill?" Liam asked.

"Well, yes," Evelyn said, "but it feels slightly wrong to cheer for twelve-year-olds beating each other up."

"But look how happy they are!" Liam pointed to the boys on the field as they untangled themselves from the pile of tackled kids. He was right. They were nodding to each other and slapping each other on the back—the classic middle-school-boy method of showing affection.

"They're definitely having fun," Evelyn agreed.

At halftime, the group of friends ran to the bottom of the bleachers. "I don't remember inviting you here," Oliver teased.

"When did you notice us?" Aaron asked.

"As soon as the coin toss happened. I could hear Caroline yelling from down here," he said. Caroline smiled at her accomplishment.

As halftime ended, they returned to their seats. Evelyn sat by Caroline, who gave her a puzzled look.

"I could make David switch seats with you so you can sit by Liam again," Caroline offered.

Evelyn shook her head. "I've had enough overthinking lately."

The girls enjoyed the rest of the game together, watching the two teams work tirelessly to get the little brown ball across the arbitrary line. Towards the end of the fourth quarter, the score was 14-14. The Eagles won by scoring a last-minute field goal. The crowd went wild. The players tackled their teammates in excitement, and Oliver cheered on his students from the sidelines. Parents congratulated the team and wrangled their children towards the cars, and after a long and tiring game, everyone headed home.

"Did you get the score back for your test?" Liam asked, crammed in the middle seat of the car between Evelyn and Aaron.

"I got an 80," Evelyn said.

"That's good!" Aaron said. "Isn't that like the hardest math class?"

Evelyn sighed. "Yeah, it is, but I think I could have done better."

Liam nodded with understanding. "You got an 80. That's a good score. Don't focus too much on what could have been. Focus on what is."

Friday, October 11

For the first time in four years of school, Evelyn entered a new boba shop. After Piper disappeared and the rude girl took her place, Evelyn didn't feel like returning to her normal store.

The new boba shop was bright, the walls covered in twinkle lights and purple butterflies. Pop music played in the background. Almost every table was packed with people, mostly high schoolers. The guy behind the counter waved at Evelyn as she entered. "What would you like to drink?"

"Can I get a strawberry green tea with crystal boba?" she asked.

"We don't have crystal boba. We have tapioca and a few flavors of popping boba." He pointed to the options on the menu above him filled with colorful letters in a wacky font.

"I'll try the mango one."

"Coming right up!" He started making her drink as she swiped her card. Two kids ran past, bumping into Evelyn's legs as they chased each other. The bell above the door dinged as a new group of teenagers walked in, two girls gossiping loudly about school drama and dragging along two boys whose expressions made it clear that they were not there of their own free will. Evelyn took her drink, thanked the employee, and walked out the door. This was not a good study spot.

She missed her old boba shop. More importantly, she missed Piper. She had never really considered Piper a friend, but maybe that was a mistake. Her Fridays weren't the same without Piper's excited greeting, the way she memorized Evelyn's order, the way she always asked about Evelyn's life and shared about her own, like they were childhood best friends catching up after a long time apart. She missed Piper dearly.

She missed Erica, too.

Losing a friend was a pain hard to describe. She had been a good friend to Erica, a mentor in a sense, and now Erica despised her, all over a stupid boy. Evelyn wanted to punch Beckett. She knew she never would—she wasn't the violent type—but she wouldn't be angry if someone else ran their fist into his face. He had manipulated her friend, and now she was gone. Erica, just like Piper, was no longer a part of Evelyn's life, and there was nothing she could do about it.

Saturday, October 12

Work was uninteresting as usual. Evelyn took a printed copy of the transcription from Melanie's recording and worked on adding a conclusion and editing the words. By the end of the day, it was far from perfect, but it was much improved.

"Good morning, Ms. Evelyn," Mr. Alfred said as he passed the front desk. He pointed at the papers in her hand. "What's that?"

"My personal statement for applications. It's a little harder than I anticipated."

He laughed. "It's good practice. Lawyers write a lot. Did you get your LSAT score back yet?"

She nodded. "166."

"You almost beat my score," he said as he walked towards the elevator.

"Wait, sir, what was your score?"

"167." He stepped into the elevator, and the doors closed in front of him.

An hour later, Evelyn packed up her belongings and left the office. The drive home was peaceful. There were cars on the road but not enough to cause traffic. She followed the other drivers like a fish in the river, letting the current take her at whatever speed it desired. Her phone played calm piano music, a playlist she had discovered yesterday after a long bout of searching for something similar to the music in the old boba shop. She thought about the boba shop, her meeting with Oliver, the words he said as he walked out the door. She thought about Liam, their close friendship, his supposed crush. She remembered the way he comforted her as he drove her to the ER with a sprained ankle, the way he answered every high-maintenance request while she was there, the way he held her hand as the doctors placed the dreaded IV in her arm. She flashed back to older memories. The friend group sat at a table in the cafeteria, laughing some days, crying others. It was the same table that she had sat at with Erica only a few weeks ago, back when they were friends. She recalled the day she first met Erica at the beginning of the semester on the sidewalk. Erica asked her for directions to the elusive science building that every freshman struggled to find. They walked and talked and exchanged phone numbers. She invited Erica to book club, and that's where they met Beckett and Melanie. Evelyn thought Melanie was annoying and dramatic, but she turned out to be wrong. Melanie was a good friend, and for that, Evelyn was grateful. She needed a stable friend amid the chaos while Piper was gone, Erica was spiteful, and Liam was enigmatic.

Life had never felt so hopeless and confusing. Evelyn found contentment only in the certainty that tomorrow was Sunday, that the sun would probably rise, and that her friends would gather as always to play a game with a story much more adventurous than her own.

Clarissa Amica

Strength	Agility	Intelligence	Intuition	Charisma
3	8	12	13	16

Health: **36**   Armor Class: **13**   Damage Dice: **d6**

Weapons:

Dagger – Use strength to hit in melee and agility to hit at range. Roll 2 damage dice for impact.

Spells:

Message – Telepathically send a message under 30 words to a person you know. They can respond with up to 30 words.

Knife – Throw a shard of energy at a person or creature you can see. Use intuition to hit. Roll 2 damage dice for impact.

Shield – Create a spherical force field around you or another person within 60 feet. The shield had a radius of 5 feet. Nothing can penetrate the shield while it's active, and no harm can be caused to the shielded person or anyone/anything else inside. If the shield is hit with a single attack worth at least 20 points of damage, the shield breaks and the spell ends.

7

Sunday, October 13

Elijah, Jareth, Derek, and Clarissa wandered the city in hopeless search of Jemma. Jareth cast a few message spells, but to no avail. By now, the sun was gone entirely, and the city was cloaked in darkness, creating the perfect atmosphere for Jemma to hide. Finding her would be a time-consuming task.

Finding Scraps, however, was easy. He ran towards them, flailing his arms in the air and screaming to get their attention. At the sight of the crazed child, Clarissa grabbed Jareth's arm and started to cast a shield spell around both of them. "Relax," Derek told her. "He's just a harmless kid, a friend of Jemma's."

Scraps tugged on Elijah's jacket. "Mr. Eli, Jemma got kidnapped! I saw it happen! We have to go save her!"

"Who kidnapped her?" Eli asked.

"Someone from the Red Coin." Scraps whispered the name like it was forbidden.

"What's the Red Coin?" Jareth asked.

"That's the guild you stole those scrolls from."

Clarissa turned to Jareth. "How are we supposed to find them?"

"Eli and I infiltrated their base once already," Jareth said.

Elijah nodded. "We'll sneak in the back entrance like last time. Derek, if they notice us, I need you to cause a distraction. Stealth is our priority, and distraction is a backup plan, but if we have to fight, we will. Clarissa, if it comes to it, let us handle the combat. I need you to use the chaos as an opportunity to find Jemma. We can split up two and two."

Jareth nodded to Elijah. "I'll go with Claire and you go with Derek."

"No!" Derek and Eli protested at the same time.

"We can't leave the two spellcasters in the same group," Eli explained. "We already made that mistake once today. I'll go with Clarissa. You go with Derek," Eli told Jareth.

"I can make the four of us invisible," Jareth offered. Elijah nodded in support.

Scraps carefully counted the number of people on his fingers. "But there's five of us."

"You're not coming with us, kid," Derek told him.

"Jemma is my friend! I can help!" Scraps insisted.

Derek shook his head. "Absolutely not."

Scraps tried to punch him in anger, but Derek caught his wrist.

"I want to go on the mission!" Scraps demanded.

Clarissa knelt down beside the kid and placed her hands on his shoulders. "Actually, I have a very special job for you. It's very important. Can you help me?"

Scraps nodded profusely.

Clarissa smiled. "Great. This is crucial to our mission, so listen carefully. I need you to go back to Artemis and let him know what happened to Jemma. Run as fast as you can. Okay?"

"Okay!" Scraps said. "Now?"

"Now."

Scraps sprinted off without another word.

Clarissa stood up. "Let's go find our friend." Jareth cast an invisibility spell, and suddenly, Clarissa was alone. The only proof of her friends' presence was the feeling of Elijah's hand holding hers.

The peaceful silence was now unnerving. She could sense Eli leading her, but she couldn't see him or the others. They paused in an alley. "We go through the door here. Jareth, message us if something goes wrong. If you get separated, meet back here outside," Eli said. The door seemingly opened on its own. Eli pulled Clarissa through, and the door softly closed.

The hallway they stood in was empty and dim, with sparse lanterns on the walls emitting a magical light. Clarissa cast a message spell to Eli. 'We can talk telepathically instead of speaking out loud.'

'That's helpful. Tell Jareth to go down to the basement. We'll check this floor.'

She sent the message as they headed down the dark hall. It opened up to a larger room, illuminated only by magical lights woven through the rafters. People were packed with barely enough space to breathe, but no one seemed to mind. A small band on a corner stage blared music throughout the room. Alcohol was consumed as quickly as oxygen. Friends and strangers drank together, laughed together, and danced together.

'Derek would love this place,' Clarissa told Elijah.

'That's why I sent them to the basement,' Eli said. 'See the large set of doors across the party? We can access the rest of the guild base through there.'

'So we have to get through this crowd without bumping into anyone. Seems impossible.'

'Basically, yes. But we have to try.' Eli started pulling her through the crowd before she could protest.

It was a bit like a dance, ducking through the crowd, dodging arms and legs, all while trying to keep hold of Eli's hand. She brushed past silk dresses and linen cloaks, hoping that her touch would go unnoticed in the commotion. They reached the other side of the room, and at just the right moment, slipped through the door without anyone discerning an invisible force opening it.

Unfortunately, they didn't account for people on the other side of the door. They entered a foyer dimly lit by lanterns, with a few guild members wandering about. Most were oblivious, but the two closest teenage boys stared at the door with curiosity. "Did you see that door move, Kai?"

Kai shrugged. "People come and go from the party. What's the big deal?"

"It moved by itself!"

"You're crazy, Finn. Doors don't move by themselves."

"I'm telling you, there's some kind of magic stuff going on," Finn insisted. He inspected the door. "Go get Ember. She can check it out."

Kai rolled his eyes. "Ember doesn't have time for your stupidity."

While the boys were busy arguing, Eli and Clarissa crept far away from the door. 'Do we start with the hallway on the right or the left?' Clarissa asked.

'Ember's office is to the left, so let's start on the right and pray they don't call her.'

They headed down the hall on the right, grateful for its vacantness. The crowded gathering was a stressful obstacle, but it kept the guild members out of their way. Clarissa and Eli peeked inside doors in the hallway. There were offices, meeting rooms, and armories, but no tied-up friends to be found.

The basement was a different story. Jareth wandered through aisles of supplies: barrels of water, boxes of food, and piles of tents and sleeping bags.

"We could restock our backpacks here and no one would even notice," Derek whispered.

Jareth sighed. "We're here for friends, not supplies."

They walked through the large warehouse until they reached the back wall. "I guess she's not down here," Derek said.

Jareth shook his head and knelt down to investigate the scrapes on the floor leading to the brick wall. He dragged his hand along the bricks, his other hand dragging Derek with him, until he suddenly paused.

"It's a wall, Jareth, what are you—"

He pushed his hand onto the wall, and a small panel clicked inwards. A hidden door in the wall slid open. 'That's what I was looking for,' Jareth said through a message spell.

'Alright, you solved the puzzle,' Derek said. 'Now I get to fight someone.'

They snuck through the open doorway, prepared for a confrontation, but there were no guards in view. The room was dark and dingy, with dirt and dried blood covering the floor. The walls were lined with cells, all but one unlocked and empty. In the back corner sat Jemma, bloodied and asleep.

"Jemma," Derek whispered, "wake up!" She stirred, but her eyes didn't open.

'Can you pick the lock?' Jareth asked.

'I can try.' Derek knelt by the lock, trying to open it, but his only knowledge was from watching Jemma perform the task. He stood back up after a few minutes. 'I can't do it.'

"Jemma!" Jareth tried again to get her attention. Derek took a granola bar out of his backpack and threw it at her, hitting the side of her head. Jareth dropped the invisibility spell on himself and Derek as she awoke.

"Hey, no, stop hurting me." Her eyes fluttered open. "Who's there? What do you want?" It took a second for her vision to focus and decipher the identity of her visitors. "Jareth! Derek! You came to rescue me!" She limped towards the edge of the cell.

"We're trying, but we can't unlock the door," Jareth said.

"That's my specialty! I just need my..." She reached in her front pockets, back pockets, jacket pockets. "They took my lock-picking tools, my daggers, my money, everything!"

Derek handed her his lock-picking set. She reached her hands through the bars and blindly picked the lock in seconds.

"You need to teach me to do that," Derek said.

"Sure, but first, we find my stuff."

"I don't care about your stuff," Jareth said. "We need to get out of here."

Jemma rolled her eyes. "Fine. Then you're buying me new weapons."

'We found her! Headed back to the meeting spot now.' A message from Jareth came through to Clarissa. She relayed the news to Elijah.

'Great,' Elijah said. 'We just have to sneak back through the party. I don't want to risk leaving through the front entrance.'

They headed back to the foyer. Finn and Kai were gone, making it easy to re-enter the party. They danced through the crowd towards the dark hallway across the room. Four silhouettes stood blocking the exit. As Elijah pulled Clarissa down the hallway, the figures came into view: Jemma, Derek, Jareth, and a girl with her arms crossed, leaning against the door. She was dressed in all-black tight-fitting clothes with an oversized cloak whose hood shadowed her face. Daggers hung from her belt, shrouded by a dark magical aura. "Did you really think you were going to take my prisoner that easily?" she asked.

"She's not your prisoner," Derek said. "She's our friend."

"I'm well aware who she is, although I'm not sure who you are." She spoke to Derek before turning to Jareth. "I know you, Jareth Amans. You stole from me once already. I won't let you fool me twice, but I will offer you a deal. Return my prisoner, and I'll let you go."

Jareth shook his head. "No way."

"Let us go, and give me my stuff back," Jemma demanded. The girl eyed Jemma like a wolf watching a puppy bark.

'Who is that?' Clarissa asked Elijah telepathically.

'Ember.'

Her eyes shot up. She stared past Jareth, into the vacant hallway where Clarissa and Eli stood invisibly. "I see you brought more friends, Jareth, although they're not as smart as you." She smiled. "I can intercept messages. It comes in handy often. I don't appreciate being deceived."

'Drop the spell,' Clarissa told Jareth. Once visible, she stepped towards Ember. "We don't appreciate being deceived either. We were told you stole the scrolls from Kinsley, so we were simply returning them. It turns out that we were lied to. You're welcome to steal them back from her; we won't stop you. We didn't ask to get caught in this crossfire. It seems you've already raided Jemma's pockets. Consider our debt paid, and let us go."

Ember glared back at her. "What you stole is worth at least double what I took from Jemma. Besides, there's more than coins at stake. Those scrolls contain powerful spells. In the wrong hands, they could wreak havoc on an entire city."

"Kinsley cares most about the appearance of status and power. She tries to sound intimidating, but she's not looking to cause mass destruction." Clarissa handed over her own stash of gold coins. "Here. This is all I have. Take it, and let us leave. You gain nothing from hurting us."

Ember took the money and stepped aside. "Don't come back to this town."

Monday, October 14

Evelyn and Melanie entered the library for book club together. It was strange to Evelyn how quickly they'd become friends. Mutual despise was an effective catalyst for friendship.

"Have you heard anything from Erica lately?" Melanie asked.

"Not since last week." Evelyn sighed. "I don't know if I have the energy to deal with them in book club today."

"Then don't. It's a club. It's not like attendance is required."

"What else would I do?" Evelyn asked.

"I know a good coffee shop south of campus," Melanie recommended.

They found Melanie's car in the busy parking lot and drove to a peaceful little coffee shop. Evelyn ordered her classic vanilla cold brew and sat down at a table in the corner. Melanie sat across from her with a cup of tea.

"How's the book going?" Evelyn asked.

Melanie sighed. "It's ok. Editing is hard, and marketing is harder, but my beta readers love the story. That's what's keeping me motivated."

"Speaking of beta reading, I finished the book." Evelyn pulled out the manuscript and handed it to Melanie. The previously pristine white pages were now covered in red and blue pen marks and the occasional coffee stain.

Melanie's eyes lit up with excitement. "Did you like it?"

"I stayed up until 2 a.m. last Tuesday because I couldn't put it down. It was a nice escape from reality."

Melanie smiled, set down her tea, and looked up at the ceiling. "Sometimes I wish I could just live in the world of my book. Being a student is boring. Being a fantasy protagonist trying to save the world is much more interesting."

"So much more interesting," Evelyn agreed.

Tuesday, October 15

As Evelyn drove home from the grocery store, her phone rang. She answered the call. "Hey, Mom!"

"Hi, Evie! How was your day?" her mom asked.

"It was good. Nothing exciting. I'm just headed home from the store."

"And how are the law school applications?"

She sighed, apparently loud enough to be audible over the phone.

"I'm sorry, honey. I don't want to bother you about it—I'm sure it's stressful—but I couldn't help but ask."

"It's okay, Mom. It's going fairly well, actually. I almost have my personal statement done. I just need a couple of people to proofread it, and I'll start submitting applications."

"That's great!" her mom exclaimed. "I'm so proud of you. Avery is too. She keeps asking me if you got accepted into law school yet. She doesn't understand that it takes time."

"When she applies to college herself in a couple of years, she'll understand. Is she passing geometry?"

"Barely. I told her to call you, but she thinks she's too cool to call her big sister for help."

"When she was little, she used to think I was the cool one," Evelyn said.

"That was before you went to school for math," her mom teased.

"Hey, I think math is cool!" she argued. "Today in class we proved how many topological holes are in a t-shirt."

"You are the only person in the world who thinks that sounds fun."

"I bet Liam thinks it's fun, so that makes at least two people." She parked her car and grabbed a couple bags of groceries, lodging her phone between her ear and shoulder.

"Who's Liam again? Is he the business major?"

"No, that's Aaron. Liam graduated already. He's the accountant."

"Right, the accountant. No wonder he has bad opinions about math."

Evelyn laughed. "Alright, Mom, I have to go. I need to help my roommate with something."

"Bye, Evie! I love you!"

"Love you too." She hung up the phone as she opened the door to the apartment.

Bethany was sitting on the rug in the living room, surrounded by pages full of scribbles. "Evelyn, I have no clue what I'm doing. My stupid test is tomorrow."

"I know." Evelyn looked down at the problems. "You're supposed to calculate the surface area of the revolution."

"I know what all those words mean independently," Bethany said, "and no clue what they mean together."

"I can show you"—she held up the bag of groceries—"and then we can make blueberry muffins."

Evelyn joined Bethany on the living room floor, surrounded by highlighted textbooks and pages of scribbled notes. The two girls studied late into the night, forsaking sleep for studying and dinner for muffins.

Wednesday, October 16

Liam:

> *i got the sequel game in the mail today! what are you guys doing tonight?*

David:

> *Game night sounds fun*

Liam:

> *how does my apartment at 6pm sound?*

David:

> *Sounds good to me*

Aaron:

> *Do I get free food?*

Liam:

> *you can eat the leftovers in my fridge.*

Aaron:

> *I'll be there*

Caroline:

> *I can bring pizza!!!*

Aaron:

> *Then I'll definitely be there!*

Evelyn:

> *I'll come too*

Oliver:

> *i'll come if we get to attack caroline with nerf guns again*

Liam:

> *deal*

Aaron:

> *Absolutely*

Caroline

> *I didn't agree to this!*

David:

See you at 6 :)

Evelyn was the first to arrive at Liam's apartment. He sat on the floor, surrounded by game pieces in tiny plastic bags. "Do you want to help me set up?" he asked.

"Sure." She sat down with him on the floor. He handed her a sheet of perforated cardboard tokens. She popped each one out of the page and sorted them by color.

"What's your favorite genre of books?" he asked.

She laughed. "Is that your conversation starter? Not 'how was your day' or 'how are your classes' or 'how are law school applications going'?"

He shrugged. "I figured you get asked those questions a lot."

"You're not wrong." She sorted the tokens into the appropriate colored baskets. "I like anything with immersive world-building and well-built characters. Typically, that's fantasy, but I read other genres too."

"Do you like dystopia?" he asked.

She shook her head. "It's too unrealistic."

He laughed at her paradoxical opinions. "So you like fantasy and realism?" he teased.

She rolled her eyes in response. "It's not very interesting when the main character beats the corrupt government every single time. It's even less interesting when the main character is a twelve-year-old girl trying to act like a middle-aged woman and the villain is pure evil with no motivation. Stories like that make it impossible to relate to the characters."

Liam looked up at her with a smile. She kept her head down, focused on the game pieces. "What's your favorite book?" Liam asked.

"That's like asking you what your favorite board game is. It's an impossible question."

"Fair enough." He handed her another sheet of tokens as she finished the first. "What's your favorite genre of food? Wait, not genre, I meant type, like cuisines, like—"

"I like Italian. I feel like you can't go wrong with breadsticks and pasta."

"I like Italian too. I'm pretty boring though. I just order chicken alfredo every time."

"You have to be more creative than that!" Evelyn argued.

"I never know what half the words on the menu even mean!" he argued back.

"Just order something random. It'll probably taste good."

He grinned. "I'll have to try that sometime."

"Alright, my turn for questions," Evelyn said. "What kind of books do you like?"

"I haven't read a lot lately, but I was trying to get back into it. That's why I asked for your favorite book."

"Wait, you want book suggestions? I have so many! Have you ever heard of—"

Their conversation was interrupted as Caroline burst through the door with pizza. "I come bearing gifts!" she shouted. David followed behind her.

As if summoned by pizza, Aaron showed up next, followed by Oliver a few minutes later. Once everyone had a plate full of food, they sat down and started the game. They played the same colors as before; Evelyn reclaimed her title as leader of the Scarlet Rebellion and inevitably teamed up with Liam once again. Caroline and David joined forces as well, determined to not let Evelyn and Liam beat them this time. In the end, neither of the pairs won. Oliver had been slowly plotting in the background, waiting for the right opportunity to strike.

"I won! I did it!" He accidentally knocked over his basket of pieces in his excitement.

"I thought you didn't like strategy games," Aaron said.

"I like them when I win."

David and Caroline worked on cleaning the kitchen while Aaron and Oliver tried and failed to escape the apartment without being noticed. Evelyn helped Liam sort the pieces back into the box and pack the game away. He smiled as he handed her the board. "Thank you for your help."

She smiled back and shrugged. "It's the least I can do. Thanks for letting everyone meet at your apartment."

He closed the box to the game and took a deep breath. His eyes lingered on the box for a second before drifting up to meet hers. "Evelyn, would you want to—"

Nerf bullets hit her shoulder, her leg, her forehead, seemingly all at once. She screamed and hid under a blanket, utilizing the thin layer of fabric as an ineffective shield. Oliver and Aaron laughed together as Caroline, their next victim, screamed too.

"Alright, children, calm down," David said. Evelyn peeked out from under the blanket as David stole the Nerf gun from Aaron and began attacking Oliver. Suddenly she was caught in the crossfire. She ran behind the couch and ducked. Liam hid with her.

"Why did we pick such crazy friends?" Liam asked.

Evelyn's voice was muffled by the blanket. "Every day with these idiots is an adventure."

Saturday, October 19

The office was always a stark contrast from campus. Every day at work was peaceful and serene. Evelyn set her purse on her desk, picked up a couple of papers, and headed to visit Mr. Alfred.

His office sat in the corner of the building. Glass stretched from the floor to the ceiling, forming the type of windows on the top floors of a city skyscraper, except the third-floor small-town view was woefully unimpressive. The remaining walls held abstract art that Evelyn could never afford but could probably paint herself. In the middle of the room sat two large chairs facing a desk where

Mr. Alfred sat working. Evelyn knocked on the door and entered once he motioned for her to come in.

She sat down nervously and handed him a couple of papers. "Would you mind reading my personal statement for me?" she asked. It was a small favor that would take only a few minutes, yet her heart pounded in her chest, pumping adrenaline through her veins as if her life depended on it. He nodded without a second thought and took the papers from her. It took all of her strength to sit still as he read it.

"This is great," he said after a few minutes. Her shoulders instantly relaxed. "Where are you applying to?"

"Harvard, Yale, Stanford, and Columbia to start with. I need a couple of safe schools too. I'm also looking at scholarships, but I know those can be hard to get, and my LSAT isn't as high as I wanted it to be. But I'm hoping if I apply to multiple schools, at least one will give me some financial aid."

"You know there's a law school down the street, right? Why don't you go there?" he asked curiously.

"It's not as prestigious as other schools, and I need a good school on my resume to get a good job after graduation."

Mr. Alfred shrugged. "I'd hire you."

Evelyn's professional demeanor shattered, and she almost jumped out of her chair. "Wait, what?"

"If those big-city lawyers you look up to won't hire you because of what school you went to, it's their loss. You're a bright and hard-working student."

"If I went to law school here, would you really give me a job?"

He shrugged again. "Sure, but you're not getting any special privileges. You'd start as a first-year associate just like everyone else."

She held back her child-like excitement, but she couldn't contain her smile. "I wouldn't ask for anything more, sir."

He handed back her personal statement. "Finish your applications. If you decide to stay in town, you can keep your job here while you're in school and start networking before you even graduate. I can try to help you get some scholarships too. I have a few friends I can call."

She took the papers and stood up. "Thank you so much."

"Good luck, Ms. Evelyn." He turned back to his computer as she walked out the door.

She dropped the facade of professionalism on the car drive home, shouting with excitement and tearing up with joy. Maybe her dreams weren't shattered after all. Maybe Oliver was right. Maybe she had been too focused on the missed opportunity to notice the ones available right in front of her.

When I was twelve years old, my little sister experienced what she believed to be the biggest injustice the world had ever seen when the Happy Hearts cereal stopped including blue hearts. The blue ones were her favorite and removing them was, in her words, a disgrace to humanity. Like any typical six-year-old experiencing a minor inconvenience, she threw a tantrum. I tried my best to console her, but she wouldn't stop screaming. Suddenly, she had a genius idea: I could sue the cereal company.

Even as a child, I understood that this wasn't a valid cause for a lawsuit, but my sister didn't accept this as an answer. I instead tried to argue that I couldn't sue them because I wasn't a lawyer, but she didn't accept my new argument either. She told me I needed to become the "bestest lawyer in the world". I quickly dismissed her idea as an impossibility.

As I grew up, I started learning about all the real injustices in the world. I began to think that maybe my little sister was right. I truly could help people as a lawyer: not kids with bad cereal, but people with real, life-altering problems. There are so many who have been unfairly hurt by the world. As a lawyer, little by little, case by case, I can play a small part in helping right the wrongs of society.

8

Sunday, October 20

E velyn sat in front of her computer, staring at the "Submit" button at the end of the law school application. The button stared back, daring her to press it. She had filled out every piece, read and reread her personal statement, and triple-checked every word of the application. Finally, she mustered up the courage to press the daunting button. The submission confirmation screen popped up, a sign of a job well done—or at least done. She moved on to the second application, then the third. Each "Submit" button was slightly less intimidating than the last. She marked each school off of her to-do list, one by one, until the seventh and final application was completed. She glanced at the clock. It was almost time for dinner with friends, and she hadn't even eaten lunch.

She drove through her favorite 24-hour taco shop and headed to David's house. For once, Oliver's insistent question about law school applications didn't scare her. She walked into the house carrying a paper bag of food and took her normal seat between Liam and Caroline.

"Are those tacos?" Liam asked.

She nodded. "I forgot to eat lunch."

Oliver rolled his eyes. "You sound like my middle schoolers on the weekends. Apparently, they're so busy playing video games that they forget to eat."

Evelyn stared Oliver down as she unwrapped her taco. "Well, I wasn't playing video games. I was finishing law school applications."

His eyebrows raised. "Really?"

She nodded. "I finished all seven," she said before taking a bite of her taco.

"Are you relieved to be done or nervous about the responses?" Liam asked.

"A little bit of both, but mostly relieved." She spoke through a mouthful of food.

"Good job, princess," Oliver said.

David took the last open seat at the table. A scheming grin spread across his face. "Let's get started."

Jemma skipped down the road while the rest of the team dragged behind, fighting to keep their eyes open and feet moving. Dawn began to break, yet the group hadn't slept one bit.

"We've been awake for too long. We need rest," Jareth said.

Eli shook his head stubbornly. "We need to keep moving. Ember said to get out of town, and I want to get far away from that girl."

Derek kicked a rock farther down the road, the same rock he'd dragged all the way from Illia. "I'm tired."

"Me too," Clarissa said.

Jemma did a cartwheel in the middle of the road. "I'm wide awake!"

"That's because you took a little nap in that cell without us," Jareth told her.

"Is that why it's called kidnapping? Because you get to take a nap?" Derek asked.

"You're too tired to be funny," Clarissa told him. "Elijah, can we please just rest?"

"Fine," Eli surrendered. He led the group off the road through some trees into a clearing. By the time he finished pitching the first tent, Clarissa was already asleep in the grass.

The group woke up a few hours later, covered in dirt and sweat. The clouds had abandoned the sky, making the heat miserable. They packed up camp and walked slowly, yet as fast as they could manage. The prospect of returning to their hometown kept them moving forward. Jareth missed his parents, Derek missed his friends, Elijah missed his son, and Jemma missed whatever hooligans she hung out with on the weekends.

Clarissa heard rustling in the bushes ahead. "Please don't let it be wolves again," she mumbled under her breath. Elijah unsheathed his sword and Derek nocked an arrow milliseconds before the pack of wolves jumped out. The team fought back with everything they had: swords and arrows and daggers and magic. Clarissa cast a spell to attack the closest wolf once, twice, three times, hurting it little by little. Despite its injuries, the wolf lunged at her. She cast a shield spell and sighed with relief when, to her surprise, the spell was successful. The wolf rammed into the transparent dome, then paused in a daze, giving Derek ample opportunity to shoot an arrow through it. Clarissa dropped the shield spell to attack her next victim, but Jareth beat her to it, and another wolf dropped to the ground. Fueled by adrenaline, Clarissa's eyes darted around the scene, looking for the next wolf, determined more attacks would come, but only silence remained. The battle ended just as quickly as it started.

"Is anyone hurt?" Derek asked. Everyone shook their heads.

Jareth hugged Clarissa. "You cast the shield spell!" he said excitedly.

She smiled back at him and took his hand. "I had an excellent teacher."

Elijah took a few more steps towards their destination. "Let's keep moving, then."

Derek found his rock and resumed his kicking. It bounced down the road sporadically, hitting other rocks and grass before resting in the dirt. Derek stepped forward and swung his foot at it again.

Jemma skipped down the road, still wide awake, energized by nothing but her own carefree attitude.

Clarissa was a little tense as they continued walking, but for the most part, Jareth's presence beside her relieved her worries. She was grateful they could keep moving, unimpeded, uninjured, and only slightly uneasy.

Jareth held Clarissa's hand tight, thankful that, for once, there were no physical threats holding their thoughts captive.

Hours turned into days. The sun painted the sky with light in the day, and the stars sprinkled the sky with light in the night. Clarissa lay on her back on the last night of their journey, staring at the stars. Jareth lay beside her.

"What happens when we get back to Mistcoast? Do we just go back to our old, boring lives?" Clarissa asked.Jareth shook his head. "There's nothing boring about life, Clarissa. Mistcoast might not have dragons to fight and epic quests to complete, but there are ships to repair and parties to attend and cupcakes to keep out of Jemma's thieving hands. There are plenty of people to love and care for. Life can be interesting without fanatical expeditions. Every breath—"

"Since when are you such a wise man?" Clarissa laughed and rolled over to look at him through the tall grass.

He smiled at the stars. "Every breath we take is a journey itself."

They woke up the next morning with air in their lungs and eagerness in their steps as they journeyed farther east. The sun ahead outlined a small scattering of buildings. A collective smile spread across their faces. They were almost home.

"We'll play one more time next week, and that'll wrap up the game," David announced.

"What do we do after that?" Evelyn asked. They had been telling the same immersive story for months. Clarissa was Evelyn's escape from reality. What was she supposed to do without that?

"We all go our own ways and never see each other again," Aaron joked.

"You can't get rid of us that easily," Oliver told him.

"I had a busy week last week, so I haven't put much thought into it," David said in response to Evelyn's question. "We'll figure it out. We could start another game, we could just eat dinner together on Sundays, we could—"

"Start a band!" Aaron suggested.

Caroline shook her head. "The band wouldn't last long. None of you know how to sing."

"Exactly. It's the perfect setup for our dramatic split and our epic reunion a year later."

Evelyn rolled her eyes as she packed up her dice. She had planned on leaving her friends behind when she moved for law school, but if she followed Mr. Alfred's suggestions, she wouldn't need to. She always assumed she'd have to say goodbye to everyone eventually and never considered the possibility of staying. The prospect made her smile. Her friends were one of the best parts of her life. Leaving them would be a tragedy she might not have to endure.

Maybe success—her career—wasn't the only thing that mattered.

Maybe her career wasn't the only defining factor of success.

"Evelyn, what about you?"

"What?" Evelyn snapped out of her thoughts and turned to see the guys staring at her.

"Do you want to play video games with us on Thursday?"

"I'll probably be camping out in the honors lounge to do homework. I'll see if I can get everything done in time." She slung her backpack over one shoulder. "I should head out soon."

"I should head out too. I have a busy day at work tomorrow." Liam grabbed his own bag, waved goodbye, and followed Evelyn out the door. He stopped at the edge of the front yard. "Hey, Evelyn."

"What's up?" she asked. Clearly he wanted to talk to her away from the rest of the group; he had made that obvious when he conveniently left with her. She could only imagine what he wanted to talk about. Every possibility awoke the butterflies in her stomach.

"You really should come Thursday. You'll want to be there."

She looked up at the stars and took a deep breath, trying not to let her confusion turn to anger. "You're just as enigmatic as Oliver."

"What does that mean?" he asked.

"It's a long story." She tossed her backpack in the passenger seat of her car. "I'll be there," she promised.

"If you're swamped with homework, I can bring you a vanilla cold brew, if that would help."

"A vanilla cold brew always helps." She sat down in the driver's seat. "I'll see you Thursday."

"See you Thursday. Goodnight, Evelyn." Liam walked away to his own car, leaving Evelyn alone to contemplate every word he said.

Monday, October 21

Evelyn's phone in her back pocket refused to quit buzzing during class. Like a child, it insisted on being viewed every few minutes. She tried her best to focus on the task at hand: writing every word the professor said and copying every equation he wrote on the whiteboard. She needed an A in this class. Even if she wasn't headed to an Ivy League law school, she still wasn't willing to give up her 4.0 GPA. She finally caved to her phone's insistent vibrating as she walked out of the building. She scrolled through the notifications: social media apps telling her about posts from influencers, news stations announcing the hot topic of the hour, and forgotten mobile games trying to convince her to buy fake currency with real money.

She added a new task for her to-do list: delete half the apps on her phone.

The text messages were the only notifications she truly cared about. There were three messages in individual chats:

Bethany:

> *I passed my calc test!*

> *We should celebrate! Do you want to go get boba?*

Melanie:

> *How do you feel about skipping book club again? We could go literally anywhere else. I don't care.*

Mom:

> *I love you! Avery loves you and misses you too. Have a good day! :)*

Evelyn debated her response, trying to decide between boba tea with Bethany or ditching book club with Melanie, before realizing it wasn't a binary choice. She texted Melanie.

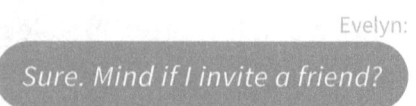

Sure. Mind if I invite a friend?

The social butterfly, of course, did not mind. They met in the parking lot at Melanie's car and, after a quick explanation, drove to pick up Bethany, who was waiting outside the dorm. Evelyn rolled down her window and waved Bethany over. Bethany hopped in the back seat with a smile on her face. "Evelyn! I made an A on my test!"

Evelyn gave her a high-five. "That's awesome!"

"I made an 87, and they added a three-point curve," Bethany said. "I'm not sure if that counts as an A."

"It definitely counts," Melanie said. "By the way, I'm Melanie. You wanted boba tea, right?"

"If that's okay with you," Bethany said.

"Of course it's okay with me!" Melanie searched for directions on her phone.

Evelyn's phone vibrated again. She ignored it at first, but it persisted. She sighed and looked to see the caller: Erica. She showed the screen to Melanie. "Should I answer?"

Melanie shrugged. "I would."

Evelyn tapped the green button and raised the phone to her ear. "Hello?"

"Hey, Evelyn." Erica sounded fragile and weak, like breathing was a laborious task. "I... I don't know why I called. I'm sorry."

"What happened?" Evelyn asked, her voice gentle and kind.

"Beckett broke up with me. I don't know what to do... I don't know why I called you. I'm sorry."

"It's okay. Where are you?"

Erica struggled to speak through tears. "In my room laying on the floor. I'm sorry. I should go."

"No, stay on the phone," Evelyn said. Melanie gave her a questioning look. She mouthed the word "Beckett", and Melanie nodded in understanding.

"What's wrong?" Bethany asked.

"Do you mind if someone else joins us?" Melanie asked Bethany in response.

Bethany shrugged. "Sure."

"We're on our way," Evelyn said into the phone. "Do you want boba tea?"

"Right now?" Erica asked. "Who is 'we'?"

"Yes, right now. I'm with Melanie and Bethany."

"Ok. I'm walking down to the parking lot," Erica said. Evelyn heard footsteps and sniffles echo through the phone.

Melanie drove to the other side of campus. Erica was easy to find, standing on the sidewalk, alone, a phone to her ear, her face red, her eyes glossy. She sat in the back of the car beside Bethany.

"Do you want to talk about it?" Evelyn asked.

Erica shook her head. "Please don't make me."

"We won't," Melanie promised. "All you need to focus on right now is breathing and boba tea." She drove through the crowded parking lot and headed towards the boba shop. Evelyn connected her phone to the car and played some music to break the painful silence. Bethany hugged Erica in the backseat while Erica cried into her shoulder.

They parked in front of the unknown boba shop and headed inside. Evelyn opened the door and was greeted by a familiar face. "Welcome to Bubbly Boba!" Piper said. "What can I get for you?"

"Piper?" Evelyn stared at her in shock.

"Hey, Evelyn!" Piper said with a smile. "Strawberry green tea with crystal boba?"

Evelyn nodded. "Do you work here now? What happened at the old place?"

Piper sighed. "I got fired over stupid drama. The manager's daughter didn't like me, and it just went downhill from there. This new job is great, though."

"Piper, who are you talking to?" An older woman limped around the corner, smiling at Evelyn.

"An old friend of mine," Piper told her. "Evelyn, this is Ms. Charlotte. She owns this place." She finished typing in Evelyn's order and turned to Melanie, who was next in line. "What would you like?"

Evelyn stepped back, letting Melanie order her drink. She noticed Charlotte's smile suddenly turn into a concerned frown. "Honey, what's wrong?" Charlotte asked, looking past Evelyn at Erica, whose red face clearly told of her past tears.

"There was a breakup," Evelyn explained for Erica.

Ms. Charlotte nodded. "Ice cream. You need ice cream. I'll be right back." She turned around and limped towards the back of the store.

Piper took Melanie's order, then Bethany's, then Erica's. Charlotte returned with a pint of ice cream and a spoon, handing it to Erica. "Back when I was in school, every time some dumb boy broke up with me or my friends, we ate a pint of ice cream. It'll make you feel better."

Erica giggled and took the ice cream. "Thank you."

"Piper, it's about time for your lunch. Why don't you take a break with your friends here? They seem nice. I like them."

"Thank you, Ms. Charlotte." Piper finished making their drinks and grabbed a paper bag with her lunch. The girls found an empty table, sat down together, and introduced themselves.

Erica was quiet for the most part, simply appreciating the ice cream and the company of the other girls, when suddenly she sighed in realization. "We're missing book club right now. I completely forgot about it."

"Do you really want to go to book club with Beckett today?" Melanie asked.

Erica shook her head. "I don't know if I ever want to go again."

"Honestly, ditching book club last week was more fun than going," Melanie said. "We don't have to go again."

"Why don't you just start your own book club?" Bethany suggested.

"Is that even an option?" Erica asked.

Melanie shrugged. "Why not? I could definitely run a book club. We just need a place to meet."

"Wait, I want to join! Why don't you meet here?" Piper said. "Ms. Charlotte won't care. Mondays are slow. She'd be happy for some consistent customers."

"Can I join?" Bethany asked.

"It was your idea! Of course you can." Melanie smiled. "This is a great idea. We're geniuses."

"And we never have to see Beckett ever again?" Erica stabbed at the ice cream with her spoon.

"Absolutely not. Don't worry about him," Melanie told her.

"You were right," Erica told Melanie, "about Beckett. You were right."

"Unfortunately, I know from experience," Melanie said. "Just eat your ice cream. You'll have plenty of time to tell me about how right I was later."

Their conversation was interrupted by the ringing of Erica's phone lying face-up on the table. Evelyn glanced over at the screen and saw Rowan's name and picture.

"He's going to kill me..." Erica said with a sigh. She looked at Evelyn. "Can you answer it?"

Evelyn picked up the phone. "Hey, Rowan."

"...who is this? Where's Erica?"

"This is Evelyn. Erica's with me," she responded calmly.

"Oh, thank goodness. I heard about the breakup, and I couldn't find Erica anywhere, and she wasn't answering my texts, and—"

"She's alright, Rowan."

"Is he mad at me for dating an idiot?" Erica whispered.

Evelyn shook her head. "Of course not. He wanted to make sure you're okay."

"Can you tell him to meet me at the library later? I want to finish my ice cream first." Erica stabbed at the dessert again with her spoon.

"She'll meet you at the library in an hour," Evelyn said into the phone.

"I'll be waiting. I thought maybe I could take her book shopping and we could go get dinner together," Rowan said. "I'm not really sure what girls want after breakups, but..."

"She'd love that," Evelyn said.

"Actually... can I talk to him?" Erica asked. Evelyn nodded and handed her the phone.

Amid all the heartbreak at the table, Evelyn smiled. It was bittersweet the way people were brought together by sadness, bonded by mutual pain. After Erica ended the call, the girls talked for almost an hour, and slowly, Erica's tears turned into laughter. They swapped stories about anything and everything that came to mind: Erica's despised chemistry professor, Piper's old dramatic job, Bethany's overprotective dad. Melanie talked about writing her book. Evelyn told about her little sister and her law school applications. They chatted about their past, their present, their future plans, their dreams that felt too unrealistic but too wanted to simply let go. The girls had all walked through their own lives, their own stories, their own plots and subplots and character arcs, all to cross paths here, at an insignificant little boba shop in a small college town. It formed a beautiful work of art as the creator of the world wove their narratives together. They left the boba shop as friends, as if they knew each other since childhood.

Piper grabbed her apron and went back to work. Ms. Charlotte waved at them from the front counter. "Goodbye, girls. Goodbye, Evelyn. Come back soon!"

Evelyn nodded. "I'll see you on Friday."

The girls drove back to campus and parted ways, walking different directions, heading towards their individual classes for their unique majors, but still connected through an invisible string of comradery and a newly formed book club group chat.

Thursday, October 24

The honors lounge, as always, was full of chaos and studying. In the midst of card games and a paper airplane contest, Evelyn sat at a table across from Melanie and worked on her psychology homework while Melanie worked on an essay. Evelyn's to-do list sat beside her, slowly but surely shrinking throughout the day, while her phone lay face down on top, buzzing, interrupting her work as always. She turned it over to see Avery calling her.

"Hey Avery!" she answered.

"Hey, Evelyn." Her little sister's response was much less enthusiastic. "What are complementary angles?"

"They're angles that add up to 90 degrees. Why?"

"What are supplementary angles?"

"Angles that add up to 180 degrees. Why? What are you doing?" Evelyn said. Melanie gave her a confused look. Evelyn covered the phone and whispered, "It's my sister."

"Geometry homework. It's due next period. I'm at lunch."

"Have you ever tried doing your homework more than an hour before it's due?"

"What's the fun in that?" Avery asked. "I work best under pressure."

"We'll see how well that strategy works for you in college."

"I don't need to go to college. I'm just going to live in your mansion after you become the bestest lawyer in the world. How's that going, by the way? What big fancy school are you going to?"

"Actually, I might stay here," Evelyn said, surprised by her own words. It was the first time she had admitted it out loud, turning an abstract idea into a definitive statement. The prospect of a less prestigious school no longer seemed like a failure. She could stay with her friends instead of starting over in a new town. She could keep her current job, and she might even have one lined up for after graduation. She could be more competitive for scholarships, and the cost of living would be significantly lower. It wasn't what she had dreamed of, but maybe her dreams were all wrong.

"Well, that's boring. You're still going to become the bestest lawyer ever, right? That's the important part."

"Of course," Evelyn said.

"Good. Okay, I should go. I have ten minutes to finish my sandwich and my homework."

"Good luck!" Evelyn said as she hung up the phone. Melanie waited expectantly. "It was my sister procrastinating on geometry homework," Evelyn explained.

"I would procrastinate too if I was taking geometry." Melanie stood up to answer a knock at the honors lounge door. Evelyn returned to her psychology homework.

"Hey, is Evelyn here?" a familiar voice asked. Evelyn put down her pencil and looked towards the door.

"Who are you?" Melanie instantly took the role of a detective.

"A friend of hers. Who are you?"

"Also a friend of hers. What's your name?"

The voice was hesitant and confused. "I'm Liam. What's your name?"

"I've never heard of you," Melanie said.

"He's a friend," Evelyn said.

"Well, in that case..." Melanie stepped aside.

Liam approached Evelyn, holding a cup in each hand. "Are all your friends so protective of you?"

"Probably just me," Melanie said, taking her seat again across from Evelyn.

THE LEGEND OF EVELYN

Liam held out a cup to her. "Vanilla cold brew."

"Did you really drive all the way to campus to bring me coffee?"

He shrugged. "I was on my lunch break, and I had nothing better to do than surprise a friend."

She took a cup from him. "Thanks. How's work going?"

"It's boring,"—he took a sip of his coffee—"but in accounting, boring is good. It means the numbers add up like they're supposed to."

"You're an accountant?" Melanie asked. "Can you do my taxes?"

"I hate taxes."

"Isn't that your whole job?" Melanie said.

"I'm guessing you're not an accounting major," Liam responded.

"English major," Melanie said.

Liam turned to Evelyn. "How's the homework going?"

Evelyn smiled. "Better, now that I have coffee."

He glanced at his watch. "I should go if I'm going to make it to my meeting on time. I'll see you tonight, right?"

She looked at the homework and sighed. "I think so. Hopefully."

He turned to Melanie. "Take good care of Evelyn, okay? Don't let her overwork herself."

"I'll try," Melanie promised.

"Bye, Evelyn." He sipped his own coffee as he walked away.

"He's cute," Melanie said, her head propped on her hand, staring towards the door even once he was out of sight. "Is he single?"

"I think he has a crush on someone."

"That's a bummer." Melanie turned her attention back to her laptop. "He seems sweet. She must be a lucky girl."

Evelyn picked up her pen and marked the last item off her to-do list with a smile on her face. She couldn't remember the last time she finished her weekly assignments by Thursday. She stared at the paper in awe, proud of the small accomplishment. By Monday, it wouldn't matter, but that wasn't important. She just wanted to enjoy the homework-free weekend while it lasted.

"What are you so happy about?" Melanie asked. "You've been smiling at a piece of paper for too long."

"I finished my homework." She tossed the paper in the trash and grabbed her backpack. "I have to go meet up with some friends."

"Will the coffee guy be there?" Melanie asked.

Evelyn nodded. "Liam will be there."

"You smiled. Why did you smile?"

"What?" Evelyn stepped towards the exit.

"You smiled when you said he'd be there! You like him!" Melanie teased.

"I never said that!" Evelyn argued, leaving the room before Melanie could insist on further discussing the topic. She walked towards the parking lot, watching the pink cotton clouds drift past the sunset. Liam had been right. Flying cars would definitely ruin the view.

Thanks to Melanie, she was acutely aware of the smile on her face and the color in her cheeks that matched the clouds.

As she drove to Liam's house, her mind started racing. What if she had it all wrong? What if Liam didn't like her? What if this was all a misunderstanding? It had to be. Of course Liam didn't like her. He wasn't an extrovert, but he was a strong proponent of intentionality. He remembered her coffee order and her favorite flavor of cake. He knew exactly how she would want to celebrate her birthday. If he really liked her, why didn't he say so? Why hadn't he asked her out?

Most importantly, why did she care? Dating was a terrifying and painful venture. She didn't want to go through that. Did she?

A small part of her did. There was a piece of her conscience that was recklessly optimistic, like an innocent child yet to learn of the evils of the world. It didn't understand the danger of its desires.

She thought back to Caroline's words, promising her that dating was worth it for the chance of falling in love.

Her memories flashed back to Alex, the first date that never yielded a second, the immediate destruction of her self-confidence. She quickly pushed that thought out of her mind.

Evelyn still believed what she told Caroline: dating was nerve-wracking and risky. The emotional vulnerability was a chance for hurt and heartbreak. That was still true, but it didn't necessarily imply Caroline's words were false. The risk might be worth it, and the only way to find out was to try, to face her fear, to go on a first date and see what happened. She dreamed of the possibilities: they could watch a movie, try a new restaurant, or even just walk around campus. They could go to a concert or an arcade or a museum or a coffee shop. Evelyn let the scenes play out in her head. In every one, in every place, right beside her, stood Liam. She couldn't imagine anyone else.

Maybe Melanie was right.

She parked at his apartment and made the long trek to the third floor. She stopped in front of the door and took a deep breath, like a student right before a job interview, like an introvert preparing to make a phone call. She knocked. After an awkward minute of silence, Liam answered. He smiled at her. She smiled back and stepped into the apartment. In the living room sat Oliver, Aaron, and David, watching her in deafening silence. The TV was dark, and the gaming controllers sat neatly on the shelf. There was no pizza, no competition, no friendly debates. It was the first time Evelyn had ever seen all four of them simultaneously quiet.

"Where's Caroline?" Evelyn asked her first of many questions.

"She's at a work event," David explained.

"What's going on here? Why do I feel like I just walked into a cult?"

"We're scheming." Aaron gave the most nondescript answer possible.

"We need your help," David told Evelyn.

"With what?"

"I need you to take Caroline to go get her nails done."

"Why?" Evelyn questioned as she opened the kitchen cabinets to search for a snack. "Nail salons stress me out, and Caroline—" She paused and swiftly turned towards David in sudden realization. "Wait, really? When?" she asked with excitement.

"Preferably tomorrow," he said.

"Okay..." Evelyn paced the small kitchen, brainstorming a plan.

"Can you do it without her figuring out?" David asked.

Evelyn nodded. "I just need to make a quick phone call." She stepped outside the apartment and dialed Melanie's number. "I need your help."

Half an hour and several schemes later, Evelyn sat on the couch beside David, with the rest of the guys standing in front of her. Her phone rang on speaker, once, twice, three times, four, until finally, Caroline answered. "Hey, Evelyn!" The road noise coming through Caroline's phone forced Evelyn to turn up the volume to hear her voice.

"Hey, Caroline! I need a favor," Evelyn said.

"Is this about Liam?"

Evelyn cringed. She kept her eyes glued to the phone, not wanting to see Liam's reaction. "No. It's about Melanie. She wants me to go with her to get our nails done tomorrow."

"That sounds like fun!" Caroline said.

"It sounds horrible! Nail salons stress me out. There are too many colors and too many options. I don't even know what half the words mean. Apparently almond is a shape, not a snack. I just don't want to look like an idiot in front of Melanie, but she really wants me to go with her tomorrow."

"Do you want me to tell you what nail design to pick?" Caroline suggested.

"Actually, I was wondering if you would come with me." The air in the room stilled as everyone held their breath.

"Sure, as long as it's after work."

There was a collective sigh of relief. "Is five o'clock okay?" Evelyn asked.

"Five is good," Caroline said. "It's a Friday; I can leave work early."

"Can you pick us both up from campus?"

Caroline laughed. "You're needy. Sure."

"Okay, I'll see you tomorrow! Drive safe!" Evelyn hung up the phone and high-fived David.

"Can we play a racing game now?" Aaron grabbed two controllers, handing one to Oliver.

David rolled his eyes at Aaron. "Liam, do you want to go shopping with me?"

Evelyn laughed. "That's not a sentence I ever thought you'd say."

Liam laughed too. "I'll come. Do you want to come, Evelyn?"

"Nope, no Evelyn," David said. "Just me and you, buddy." David placed a hand on Liam's shoulder.

Liam looked at Evelyn and shrugged. "Sorry."

"That's okay," she said. "I'll just stay here and beat Aaron in a racing game."

Aaron grabbed a third controller from the shelf and held it out to Evelyn. "Good luck. Which car do you want?"

"Pick the green one. It matches your eyes," Liam said as he walked out.

"I never noticed you had green eyes," Aaron commented.

Oliver chuckled. "Liam noticed."

"Well, of course Liam noticed," Aaron said.

"How long have you two known that he likes me?" Evelyn asked.

"I don't know what you're talking about," Aaron said.

"Me neither," Oliver said with a telling grin on his face.

"You two are the worst," Evelyn said as she picked the green race car.

"Conversations with the guys are like Vegas," Aaron told her.

"I was thinking more like Fight Club," Oliver suggested.

"I haven't seen that movie," Evelyn said. Both boys turned to stare at her in unison.

"We have a new agenda for the evening," Oliver said.

Aaron nodded. "I'll beat you two in this race first, and then it's movie night."

Liam and David returned in the middle of the movie. David propped his elbows on the back of the couch behind Aaron. "What happened to racing games?" he asked.

Aaron put his hand over David's mouth without taking his eyes off the screen. "Don't interrupt the masterpiece."

"I'd never seen this movie. They decided I needed to watch it," Evelyn said. She sat on the floor, enveloped by a large blanket, holding a bowl of popcorn. "I raided your pantry," she told Liam. She gestured to the popcorn, then looked at the blanket. "I raided your closet, too. Sorry."

"I don't mind." Liam sat beside her and stole some popcorn. "I can't believe you'd never watched Fight Club."

A piece of popcorn hit Evelyn from behind. "No talking!" Aaron insisted.

Liam threw a piece of popcorn back at Aaron. He stole a corner of the blanket from Evelyn, solidifying his seat on the floor with her, and turned his attention to the movie.

"Evelyn? Hey, Evelyn." She woke up to a gentle voice and a hand on her shoulder.

Aaron gasped. "Did you fall asleep during the movie?"

"Only the last half hour," Liam said.

"You knew she was asleep, and you didn't wake her up!" Aaron was in shock at the atrocity of missing a part of Fight Club.

"You should have just bought me another vanilla cold brew," Evelyn said.

"Caffeine doesn't treat exhaustion; sleep does," Liam argued. "Go home."

"But we need to rewatch the last 30 minutes of the movie!" Aaron said.

"We will another night," Oliver promised. He looked at David. "Big day tomorrow. Get some sleep."

"I'll try," David said as he headed towards the door.

Evelyn stood up, leaving the comfort of the plush rug and the cozy blanket. She set the popcorn bowl in the sink and carefully folded the blanket to return it to the closet. Liam opened the closet door for her. "How did your homework go?"

"It went well! I finished it all, for this week at least. I'll get drowned in another flood of assignments on Monday."

"Enjoy it while it lasts," Liam said.

Evelyn followed David out the door. "Goodnight, Liam."

"Goodnight, Evelyn."

Friday, October 25

"So who's the best friend with the crush?" Piper asked.

Evelyn almost choked on her drink. "What?"

"You know what I'm talking about," Piper said with a grin.

Evelyn sat down her cup and took a deep breath. "His name is Liam."

"Do you like him?" Piper asked.

Evelyn shrugged her shoulders, but her face gave away her secret.

Piper smiled back. "Don't worry, I won't tell." She cleaned off a few tables and went back to the counter to take more orders. Evelyn opened to the first page of her new book, finally one that hadn't been chosen for her by a club or a professor. She sipped her tea, and her shoulders relaxed. This was what peace looked like, she realized with a smile. This was what it meant to take a break.

After a few chapters, her alarm interrupted her. She wished she could stay and read forever, but there was a more important task at hand.

She found Melanie waiting for her outside the honors lounge. A bubbly smile covered Melanie's face. "I'm so excited!"

"I didn't know acrylic nails were so exhilarating," Evelyn said.

"No, not that! I'm excited for what happens after we get our nails done!" Melanie clarified.

"You haven't even met Caroline yet," Evelyn laughed. "She's going to know something is off by that grin on your face."

"I need to summon my best acting skills," Melanie said as Caroline's car pulled up to the curb. The girls both hopped in the backseat.

"Alright, kiddos, where are we headed?" Caroline asked.

"I'll text you the address," Evelyn said.

"This is going to be so much fun," Melanie said. She introduced herself to Caroline, and the two of them talked the entire drive to the nail salon. Evelyn grinned. With Melanie being such a talkative social butterfly, Caroline wouldn't get a moment of quiet to question their motives. This would be easy.

The nail salon was calm. Light instrumental music played over the speakers. Branches with blush pink flowers were painted along one wall. Above the mural, small televisions showed a young couple touring absurdly expensive houses. A few women sat in pedicure chairs, some watching the show, others chatting and laughing together. Evelyn could understand why people found it relaxing, yet the place still made her tense. She looked at the shelves of nail polish displaying at least a hundred allegedly unique shades of red.

"Evelyn, come on!" Melanie dragged her over to a table with chairs on each side. Evelyn sat down between Melanie and Caroline. The nail tech sat across from her, asking questions about what she wanted. She turned to Melanie, and then Caroline, clearly clueless about the process and overwhelmed by the options.

"Green is her favorite color," Caroline told Melanie.

"She looks good in pink too!" Melanie said, leaning forward to talk to Caroline past Evelyn. "What about some sort of floral design?" Melanie asked.

"I like that! What do you think about adding glitter?" Caroline asked back.

"I just want something simple!" Evelyn protested.

Caroline and Melanie both laughed. "Okay, I have a simpler idea," Caroline said. "What about a solid color, like a solid green—"

"That sounds nice."

"—with glitter. Sparkles are lucky, remember?" Caroline teased.

Evelyn rolled her eyes. "Sure. Green and glitter."

Caroline picked out her own nail color, a sparkly silver, and Melanie picked purple. The nail techs started their work, consistently reminding Evelyn to just relax. She was tense at first, but as she talked with Caroline and Melanie, her anxious heartbeat slowed. With no homework to worry about, no law school applications to stress over, and no drama to deal with, her shoulders relaxed. The constant storm of her thoughts began to finally calm. She closed her eyes, taking in the music, listening to Melanie and Caroline bond over complaints about inconsistent clothing sizes. The nail salon became a luxurious oasis. Her racing mind slowed.

She almost forgot about the important task ahead.

She looked down at her nails. The color was pretty, not a vibrant lime green like a neon sign or a dark forest green like shaded leaves, but a calm sage green like the cute little succulent that sat on her desk at work. The sparkles twinkled in the light like the gold flecks in her eyes in the summer.

The girls paid for their manicures and left out the door. Evelyn glanced at the time on her phone. They were right on schedule.

"Can you drop me off at the hiking trail by campus?" Melanie asked Caroline. "I'm meeting up with some friends there."

"Sure," Caroline agreed. They drove towards the park.

Melanie grinned in the backseat as she gave directions. "Turn left, then right, then just park right up there."

Caroline parked that car. "What's that about?" She pointed at the lanterns and roses lining the walking trail and hopped out of the car to investigate.

Evelyn sighed in relief. David was right. Caroline was too curious to simply drive away without exploring.

Evelyn and Melanie lingered behind, letting Caroline explore the trail ahead of them, until she reached the clearing where David stood with a small box in his hands. Caroline squealed with excitement, running up and hugging him before he even had a chance to ask the question. Evelyn stayed on the path through the trees, out of the clearing and out of earshot of David's speech, but she could see his smile as he asked the love of his life to marry him. She couldn't help but smile too.

She felt a tap on the shoulder and turned to see Aaron standing behind her. "Where are Liam and Oliver?" she asked in a hushed whisper. He pointed at two figures hidden in the trees on opposite sides of the clearing, both holding cameras.

They watched as David gave Caroline the ring. After a kiss, a hug, and a few more kisses, Caroline ran over to Evelyn and Melanie. "I'm engaged, Evelyn!" Caroline shouted, as if Evelyn hadn't watched the whole interaction.

"I'm so excited for you!" Evelyn hugged her.

"Can I see the ring?" Melanie asked. Caroline gladly showed her. The diamonds twinkled in the sunlight.

"It's so sparkly," Caroline said, mesmerized by the refractions of light as she moved her hand.

"That means it's lucky," Evelyn reminded her.

Liam and Oliver came out of their hiding spots. They high-fived each other, pleased with the success of their plans. Caroline turned around and gasped. "I didn't know you were here!"

Oliver nodded. "I got the video, and Liam took pictures."

Melanie leaned close to Evelyn and whispered, "I didn't know your cute friend had a cute friend." Evelyn rolled her eyes in response.

Liam approached Evelyn with the camera. "Do you want to see the photos?" She nodded. They sat down on a bench at the edge of the trail and looked through the photos together.

"I had no clue you were a professional photographer," she said.

He shook his head. "I'm not. I just spent all week watching YouTube videos about proposal photography."

Evelyn laughed. "David should be grateful to have such good friends."

"He is. We've been planning this for weeks now. I'm just glad it all went smoothly."

"Evelyn, David said there's cake at his house!" Caroline shouted. "We can have a party!"

"We'll drop off Melanie and meet you there," Evelyn said.

"Aaron and Oliver offered to drop me off," Melanie countered with a mischievous grin on her face. She winked at Evelyn.

"Let's go then. I want cake," Aaron said as he walked towards his car. Melanie and Oliver followed.

Liam looked at the lanterns and roses on the trail and sighed. "We were supposed to clean this up."

"David was probably a little distracted," Evelyn said with a laugh. She picked up a few lanterns and brought them towards Liam's car. He unlocked the trunk, and she started packing the lanterns. She walked back and forth down the trail, picking up lanterns, listening to the stillness broken only by the birds chirping and the leaves crunching beneath her feet. She couldn't remember the last time she walked outside without headphones.

Liam approached with a bouquet of roses he picked up from the trail. He handed them to her. "These are for you."

"I don't want to steal Caroline's flowers," she protested.

"There's six dozen roses on this trail. Caroline won't know what to do with that many flowers. Besides, David said you could take some."

Evelyn smiled and took the roses. She sat in the passenger seat of Liam's car, and he started driving. Her thoughts spiraled again. He gave her flowers. What did that mean? Was it meant to be a romantic gesture? Was he just trying to be resourceful and minimize waste? Did he even like her? Had she misinterpreted everything until this point? Did she even want to date him?

Yes, she did. She knew she did, but did he want to date her? Did he like her as more than a friend? Did he even like her as an acquaintance? He did call her a mess once, and—

"Evelyn." Her name in his voice snapped her out of her trance. "Are you okay?"

She nodded. "I'm sorry."

"Were you lost in thought?" he asked.

She inhaled, then exhaled, trying to quiet her thoughts and slow her racing heartbeat. "Yeah. I'm sorry."

"You don't have to apologize. I just wanted to make sure you're alright." There was a moment of awkward pause before he spoke again. "Your nails are pretty. They look like your eyes."

She laughed. "You like my eyes."

He nodded. "I like more than your eyes, Evelyn."

"Like my hair?" she asked nervously, immediately internally berating herself for her every word. She instinctively brushed her fingers through her blonde locks.

"I like the way you fidget with the ends when you're nervous." He gave her a smile that seemed to both calm and spark her anxiety at the same time. "I like your determination and your work ethic. I like the way you care about your friends even when calling us idiots. I like your mind. You're smart and clever and thoughtful."

"Sometimes I think I'm too thoughtful," she said.

"Sometimes I wish, for your sake, that your thoughts would shut up for a little while," Liam said. "You doubt yourself too often, but you always encourage others. I like that about you. Yes, I like your eyes, and your hair, but most importantly, I like who you are." He sighed. "I don't know why I'm telling you all of this. It's just... you're going to graduate and leave us next year, and I didn't want it left unsaid."

"Can I ask a really blunt question?" she asked.

"I'm friends with Oliver. I'm used to blunt questions," Liam said. "Go for it."

"Why haven't you asked me on a date yet?"

He paused, caught off guard by the question that was obvious to Evelyn. "You don't like dates, according to Caroline. You think of me as a friend, and I'm grateful for that. I don't want to ruin it. On top of that, you're moving next year, and you'll be busy with law school. Long-distance relationships are hard, and I don't want you to have to go through that." He stared out the front windshield, trying to focus on driving, waiting nervously for her response.

"I like you too."

They both sat in awkward silence. Liam parked in front of David's house, but neither of them stepped out of the car. They were both frozen, until finally, Evelyn spoke. "I might not be moving next year."

"Really?" Liam asked. "I thought you had your heart set on it."

"I did, but it probably won't happen. Maybe it's for the best." She let go of her hair and placed her hand over his. "Do you want to eat dinner on Monday?"

"Obviously I want to eat dinner on Monday."

She laughed and rolled her eyes. "Do you want dinner with me?"

He nodded. "Is this a date?" he asked.

She shrugged. "Do you want it to be a date?"

An uncontrollable smile spread across his face. "It's a date."

Her smile mirrored his. "A first date. One date, and we'll figure it out from there."

He looked down at their hands, her fingers intertwined in his, his thumb brushing her wrist. He looked up at her eyes, and she impulsively looked away, trying to hide her blushing. "Can I pick you up at six on Monday?" he asked.

"Sure." She looked back up at him, acutely aware of the redness in her cheeks and the wonder in her eyes. His hazel eyes stared back, awestruck, nervous, and excited all at once. Is this what he saw when he looked at her? Did he see every emotion she'd ever tried to hide? Somehow, she wanted both to sit in the moment forever and to fast forward to their date. Unfortunately, neither of those were an option. "We should go inside and join the party."

Liam's gaze lingered on her for a second longer before he unbuckled his seatbelt, stepped out of the car, and walked

THE LEGEND OF EVELYN

through the front yard towards the house. Evelyn followed behind him. Aaron opened the door and handed them each a slice of chocolate cake. "Welcome to the party!"

Oliver waited until Aaron walked away. "You two sat in the car for a while," he noted.

Evelyn nodded. "We had a nice conversation."

Oliver grinned at Liam. "Good. I'll interrogate you about it later. For now, let's go celebrate the engagement."

Evelyn sat down on the couch beside Aaron. "Who would have thought that meeting you in a miserable freshman seminar class would have led to me helping a friend propose three years later?"

Aaron laughed. "Who would have thought that me failing calculus and hiring Liam as a math tutor would lead to his friend giving me an hour-long lecture about the three C's of diamonds?"

"I'm pretty sure there's four C's," Liam said.

Aaron shrugged. "I probably listened about as well as I did in calculus class."

Evelyn rolled her eyes. "You guys are idiots," she said as David and Caroline joined them in the living room. They sat and talked for the rest of the night, retelling stories from their past and brainstorming ideas for the upcoming wedding, until the moon came out to remind them to sleep and they all headed home.

THE FRIEND GROUP

David Justin Moore - *an introverted friend and fiancé who breaks out of his shell every Sunday*
    Strengths: kindness, carefulness
    Weaknesses: shyness, uncertainty
    Skills: writing, storytelling

Caroline Elizabeth Jordan - *a hopeless romantic who listens to superstition over logic*
    Strengths: creativity, optimism
    Weaknesses: irrationality, naivety
    Skills: art, insight

Oliver Jacob Mason - *a stubborn motivator who wants the best for everyone*
    Strengths: cleverness, stubbornness
    Weaknesses: recklessness, stubbornness
    Skills: coaching, persuasion

Aaron Zechariah Anderson - *an amateur comedian who never fails to make people smile*
    Strengths: conviviality, sympathy
    Weaknesses: obliviousness, distractedness
    Skills: business, humor

Liam Christopher Matthews - *a careful listener who knows people better than they know themselves*
    Strengths: empathy, understanding
    Weaknesses: nervousness, anxiety
    Skills: logic, attentiveness

Evelyn Marie James - *an adventurous spirit who may have found the right path to wander*

Strengths: determination, thoughtfulness
Weaknesses: overthinking, perfectionism
Skills: math, organization

9

Sunday, October 27

They gathered around the table in David's house, dice and maps and notes scattered everywhere. Evelyn sat between Caroline and Liam, between her best friend and her future boyfriend. She felt a sense of belonging she'd never felt before.

She was still an overthinker. She had spent last night stressing over the upcoming partial differential equations test that would probably ruin her 4.0 GPA and the law school scholarships that she desperately needed to financially survive. Her conversation with Liam on Friday had also given her plenty of words to spiral through. Today, however, her mind was quiet. She felt at peace. She felt at home.

"We'll wrap up the game today," David announced. "Let's get started. Last we left off, you could see Mistcoast on the horizon. What would you like to do?"

They ran the last mile to Mistcoast. For once, they ran with nothing chasing from behind and with nothing they were catching ahead. It was freeing, peaceful, and maybe a slight sign of impatience.

Mistcoast welcomed them in. There were no large walls protecting the city like in Caridelle and no thieves' guilds to kidnap them like in Illia. People went about their normal day. A few recognized them and waved, but there was no commotion, no fanfare. It wasn't necessary. Traveling across Arydia, they were foreign adventurers and warriors, but entering Mistcoast, they were simply kids returning home.

"Dad?" They heard a small voice coming from nearby. Suddenly a child pushed past Clarissa and jumped into Eli's arms. "I missed you!"

Eli hugged him tight. "I missed you too, buddy. Did Aunt Sophia take good care of you?"

Tobias nodded. "She gave me lots of cookies!"

"Where did Jemma go?" Derek asked. They looked around for her, but she was gone without a trace.

"She's probably back with her conniving friends," Elijah said. "It's a small town. We'll see her eventually."

"I guess I should go say hello to people too," Jareth said.

"So that's it? We've been on this wild long adventure together. Are we really supposed to just go our own ways?" Derek asked.

"We'll still see each other," Jareth promised. "We'll meet up sometime."

Derek nodded. "Ok. I'll go find my family. I'll see you soon."

"I'll head out too. I need to check on my sister," Elijah said.

They all waved goodbye and headed separate directions: Elijah heading east, Derek heading south, and Jareth heading north. Clarissa stood still. She knew every face and name in Mistcoast, yet she called none of them family or friends. Everyone knew her name, but no one knew her. She looked around at the crowds of people. A few familiar faces waved, but no one approached her.

"Clarissa?"

She saw Jareth a block down the street. He had stopped walking to watch her.

"I'm headed to find my family. Do you want to come?" He held out an inviting hand.

She jogged down the street to catch up. With a smile, she took his hand, and they headed north together.

"That's where we'll end the game," David said with a smile.

"Let's start a new one next week," Caroline said.

"What kind of ridiculous character are you going to build this time?" Oliver asked her.

"I'm thinking of a wizard who loves baking cupcakes."

The group laughed together. They discussed new character possibilities and plot ideas late into the night, snacking on leftover cake and forgetting about their classes and jobs to attend to tomorrow. They wrote stories together—both collaborative, fictional narratives and deep, long-lasting memories.

Evelyn looked around at her chaotic friends and David's messy house. These rooms were filled with history: of joy and of sadness, of victory and of failure, of friendship, of fighting, and of reconciliation. She used to think of this place as an escape, where she could live vicariously through Clarissa and go on exciting escapades she could never experience herself. She realized now that this house, this friend group, wasn't a break from reality but a journey through it.

As she drove home, she thought of her day tomorrow: the tough class in the morning, the brand-new book club in the afternoon, and the date night in the evening. There were no scrolls to steal or dragons to fight, but she didn't need fantasy to have adventure.

Life was an adventure itself.

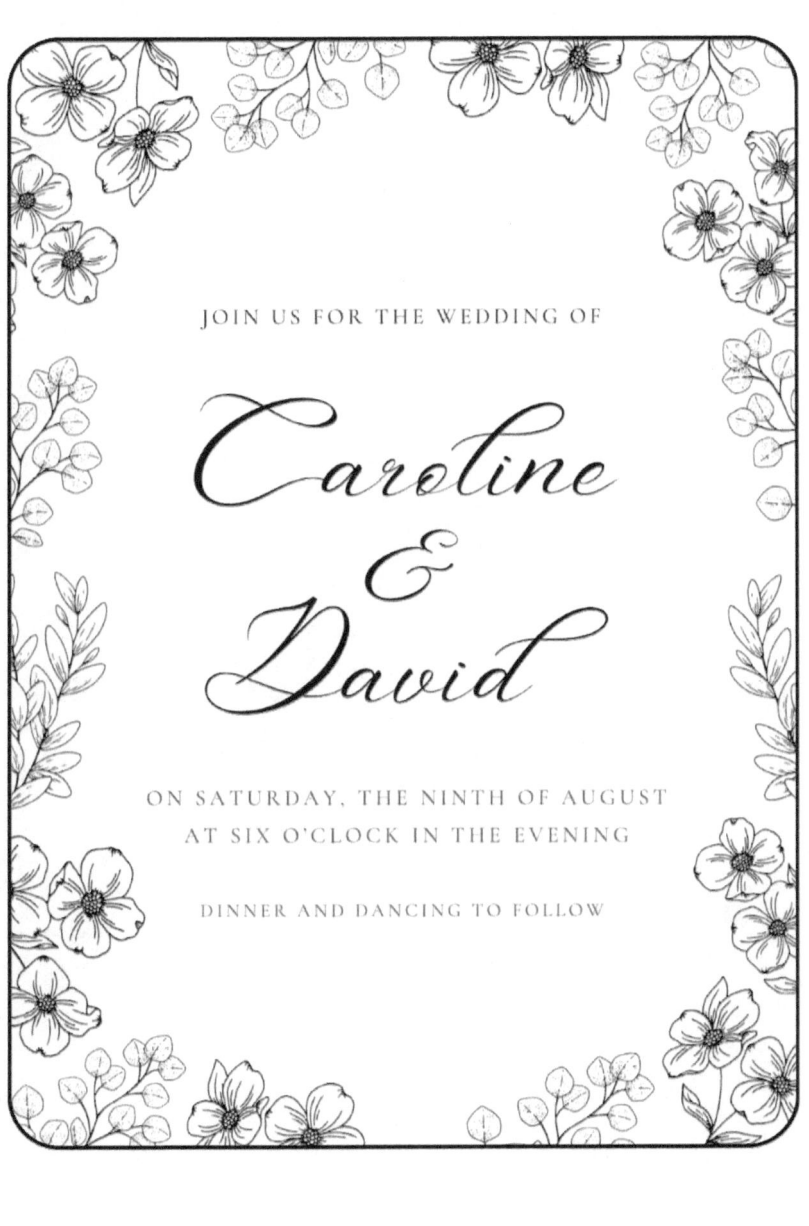

JOIN US FOR THE WEDDING OF

Caroline
&
David

ON SATURDAY, THE NINTH OF AUGUST
AT SIX O'CLOCK IN THE EVENING

DINNER AND DANCING TO FOLLOW

Epilogue
10 Months Later

Saturday, August 9

E velyn walked down the aisle, her hand resting on Liam's arm, trying her best not to trip on her floor-length scarlet dress or drop her bouquet of roses. As they reached the front of the ceremony, Liam stepped away, and she joined the rest of the girls wearing different shades of red and pink. It was a bit of an unusual choice for wedding colors, but Caroline had never cared for conventions.

Every aspect of the day was absolutely beautiful, from the bouquets of flowers to Caroline's glittery dress to the symbolism of the ceremony, which ended in the blink of an eye. Time passed by quickly, and for once, Evelyn wished it would slow. The summer had almost ended, and law school would begin soon. She still needed to move all of her stuff out of her dorm—and into her new apartment only a mile away.

She walked back down the aisle to the reception. After their big entrance, she took her seat as maid of honor next to Caroline. "How are you feeling?"

Caroline couldn't stop smiling. "It's the best day of my life."

They continued on through dinner and the first dance. As the dance floor opened for everyone, Evelyn stayed in her seat. She never cared much for dancing. Suddenly, the upbeat music changed to something slower. Liam approached and reached out his hand. "May I have this dance?"

She rolled her eyes and stood from her chair, joining him on the crowded dance floor. Liam looked over at Oliver, who was standing by the sound system. Oliver winked at him.

"You told him to ask for a slow song, didn't you?" Evelyn asked.

Liam shook his head. "It was his idea."

When she glanced back at Oliver again, he was pushing his way through the crowd to Melanie, who gladly joined him for a dance.

"You look beautiful," Liam said.

"You've already seen this dress on me like eight times. There were so many rounds of alterations."

"And you look beautiful in it every time."

She looked into his hazel eyes, not hiding her blushing from him anymore.

"Do you remember the first time we danced together?" Liam asked.

She laughed. "We kept tripping over our feet so much I was worried I would sprain my ankle."

Liam smiled. "I barely remember that part. I just remember telling you I loved you for the first time. It took me all day to build up the courage."

Evelyn rolled her eyes. "You think that was scary? Do you remember the first time I met your parents?"

"My parents are nice. I don't know why you were so nervous."

"I thought they wouldn't like me!"

"Of course they liked you! How could they not? You're amazing."

"Do you remember the time you met my mom?" Evelyn said. "You were scared too."

Liam nodded. "I think I was more scared of meeting your sister."

"My sister is a mess."

"Just like you," Liam teased. He hugged her tight, and she rested her head on his shoulder. Her eyes drifted closed, and her thoughts rolled to a stop. Despite the hundreds of people and tons of overlapping conversations, there was a strange feeling of peace with Liam's arms wrapped around her.

Time progressed too fast again, and soon, the dances finished and speeches began. Liam took the microphone first. He talked about his memories of meeting David and their interrogation of Caroline when she joined the group. He spoke of the many pieces of wisdom both Caroline and David had given him over the years. The speech was nostalgic and thoughtful, just like him.

When Liam was finished, he passed off the microphone to Evelyn. She held it in one shaking hand and her printed speech in the other. She closed her eyes and took a deep breath.

"The day I met Caroline, I knew we would become best friends. She's carefree, spontaneous, chaotic. I didn't necessarily ask for it, but she made my life much more interesting. She always knows how to make me smile when I'm having a rough day." She looked back at Caroline with a grin. "There's more to Caroline than fun and sparkles. She's kind and caring. She gives really good advice, especially if you buy her a burger and some sweet potato fries. She has always believed in me when I didn't believe in myself. She's taught me so much over the past few years. She taught me that growing up doesn't mean we can't have childish fun. She's shown me how to have joy in difficult and unpredictable times. Most importantly, she taught me about love. She convinced me that love could be more than a recipe for disaster, and through David and her, I got to witness it firsthand. They've been through so much together, but they've always loved each other. They've always put each other first. They're forgiving, thoughtful, and considerate, both to each other and to their idiotic friends. David, thank you for loving Caroline, even when I'm sure she drives you crazy at times. Caroline, thank you for loving David, and for showing me what love is. I love you both, and I'm so excited for the next chapter of your lives."

The attendees clapped as Evelyn finished her speech. She started to hand the microphone back to the emcee, but Caroline took it first. "I was told you don't talk at your own wedding, but as an extrovert, I think that's stupid." The room laughed with the bride, who turned to Evelyn with a smile. "Evelyn, you are such an amazing person. You're so sweet and kind. You're determined, maybe a little too determined sometimes. I'm still trying to teach you how to relax. You said you're grateful for us, and I want you to know that David and I are so glad we've gotten to know you. We love you dearly, as does everyone in our friend group"—she smiled—"especially Liam. You told me once that you didn't believe you're the kind of girl that will ever get married. I'm really hoping you've changed your mind. Turn around."

In confusion, Evelyn did as she was told. Liam knelt on one knee, holding a ring. He started talking about their relationship, about their love, about spending the rest of their lives together, but Evelyn could barely catch a word he said over the sound of rushing adrenaline in her veins. She remembered clearly, however, the last four words of his presentation.

"Will you marry me?"

She smiled. The adventure had only begun.

Acknowledgements

I thank God daily for giving me the strength to finish this book. It took over a year to write, edit, and publish, and the Lord has guided my every step. He's also surrounded me with an amazing team of people, and I couldn't have done this without them.

First off, thank you to my beta readers: Justin Heard, Zech Roberson, Ian Tate, Kaitlyn Carty, Sydney Short, Avery Hudgeons, David Scherm, and Jordan Frimpter. Justin, Zech, and Ian, thank you for all the game nights and crazy adventures that inspired this book. I look forward to the many more to come. Sydney and Avery, thank you for letting me be your obnoxious honorary big sister. I'm so proud to see the great people you two are growing up to be. Kaitlyn, thank you for teaching me what true friendship can look like. I don't think I could have written friends like this if I hadn't met you. David, thank you for following me, a random stranger on the sidewalk, to the BSM. Thank you for the worship jam sessions, the late night games of Sardines, and all the other college chaos that heavily influenced this novel. Jordan, thank you for being my first writing buddy, my first critique partner, and my first cheerleader. Our silly middle school stories laid the foundation for everything I write today.

Thank you, Tyler, for listening to all my stories and rants, for supporting all my writing endeavors, and for believing in me even on the days when I don't believe in myself.

Thanks to Carissa from Panera for all the smiles and sodas that kept me motivated and caffeinated as I poured hour after hour into this novel.

Thank you to all of my readers for making it this far. I hope you enjoyed reading this book as much as I enjoyed writing it.

Lastly, I want to thank my family. Alyssa, thank you for supporting me since the day you found out about the book. Mom and Dad, thank you for loving me every day and for teaching me everything I know. Tyler, buddy, thanks for always being you. I know you can't read all the words in this book yet, but it's dedicated to you, and I hope one day you'll come to love this story as much as I do.

About the author

Tessa Marie is a full time data scientist and part time author, dedicated to writing intriguing and inspiring stories across a variety of genres. When she's not writing code or books, she enjoys playing guitar, spending time with friends, and repeatedly losing to her husband in video games. Follow her writing journey (and other adventures) on Instagram: @tessa_marie_writes.